Elaine leaned closer and touched Cheryl's lips with her own. Before Elaine knew what was happening, Cheryl pulled her into her arms for a deep kiss that left them both breathless. At the mercy of Cheryl's mouth on her throat, Elaine struggled for composure. Seconds later, Cheryl's tongue became urgent and demanding. Her hands moved swiftly over Elaine's body.

"The sofa's for kids," Cheryl whispered. "Come to bed with me."

LOOKING FOR NAIAD?

**Buy our books at
www.naiadpress.com**

**or call our toll-free number
1-800-533-1973**

**or by fax (24 hours a day)
1-850-539-9731**

Those Who Wait

BY
PEGGY J.
HERRING

THE NAIAD PRESS, INC.
1999

Printed in the United States of America on acid-free paper
First Edition

Editor: Lila Empson
Cover designer: Bonnie Liss (Phoenix Graphics)
Typesetter: Sandi Stancil

Library of Congress Cataloging-in-Publication Data

Herring, Peggy J., 1953 –
   Those who wait / by Peggy J. Herring.
      p.   cm.
   ISBN 1-56280-223-2   (alk. paper)
   I. Title.
PS3558.E7548T48   1998
813'.54—dc21
                                                    98-31630
                                                    CIP

For Frankie

BOOKS BY PEGGY J. HERRING

About the Author

Peggy J. Herring lives in south Texas with her partner of twenty-four years. She enjoys reading and writing. Peggy is the author of *Once More with Feeling, Love's Harvest, Hot Check,* and *A Moment's Indiscretion.*

Chapter One

The telephone rang, jarring them both awake. Blanche, in a sleep-induced stupor, struggled out from under the covers and felt around on the nightstand for the phone.

"Hello," she mumbled.

"Phoebe?" the soft female voice said.

"No, it's Blanche. What time is it?"

"I'm sorry it's so late. This is Cheryl. Did you see Mickey at all today?"

Phoebe Carson, Blanche's now-awake lover, elbowed her in the ribs and squinted over Blanche's bare shoulder at the clock. It was three-thirty in the morning.

"Mickey? No. We haven't seen her at all this week."

"Thanks," Cheryl said. "I'm sorry I woke you."

Blanche blinked a few times as the line went dead in her ear.

"Who's looking for Mickey over here?" Phoebe grumbled. She socked her pillow in an attempt to prep it for further slumber.

"Cheryl. And she sounded upset." Blanche turned the light on and dialed Cheryl and Mickey's number from memory. It was answered on a half ring.

"Mickey?"

"No, it's Blanche again. Are you all right? What's going on?"

Cheryl sniffed, and Blanche thought she heard a sob. The tiny hairs on the back of her neck stood up, and she was grateful when Phoebe, who was always much better during a crisis, took the phone away from her.

Tossing the cover aside and scrambling out of bed, Blanche pulled on a pair of sweats and began searching for shoes.

"We're coming over," Phoebe said into the phone. "Take it easy. We'll be there in ten minutes."

They finished throwing on clothes in silence and didn't say anything until were in the car and backing out of the driveway. Phoebe's night vision was better, so she drove. Glancing at her worried lover, Phoebe reached over and took Blanche's hand.

"Mickey's probably working late and isn't answering her phone at the office," Phoebe said. *Here you go making excuses for her again.*

2

"The little shit knows better."

Blanche had a plan in mind. Once they knew where Cheryl had already called to try to find Mickey, their search would be narrowed considerably. In her heart Blanche prayed that her talented, thoughtless daughter was still at work getting a case ready instead of in some bar's parking lot passed out. No one wanted to deal with a drunk Mickey.

Phoebe rang the doorbell at Cheryl Trinidad's modest northside home. Cheryl answered it immediately. She looked a bit frayed around the edges, but she was still more elegant and attractive than anyone had a right to be at this hour.

"Hi," Cheryl said, hugging them both. Even in jeans and a Saint Mary's University T-shirt, Cheryl brought class to the simple outfit. "Thanks for coming. She'll be so angry that I called you."

"So you've heard from her?" Blanche asked, feeling a sense of relief sweeping over her.

"No," Cheryl said as she turned away from them. "I meant when she finally gets home."

"Where all have you called?" Phoebe asked. She put an arm around Cheryl's shoulder and led her to the sofa.

"The police, hospitals, her office, every friend and coworker I had a number for." Cheryl closed her eyes and rubbed her perfectly shaped nose. "Other than the police and the hospitals, all I managed to do was wake people up." She leaned her head back as tears rolled down the side of her face. "I started at eleven-thirty. The bars were closed by the time I thought of checking there." She reached over and squeezed Blanche's knee, saying again, "She'll be so angry that I called you."

Blanche, in return, gave Cheryl's hand a comforting pat. "She'll get over it. How about I make some coffee? We might be here a while."

Once Blanche was in the kitchen, Phoebe leaned over and asked, "You think Mickey could be out drinking?"

Cheryl shrugged and dabbed at her eyes with a damp, crumpled Kleenex. "I don't know. She's been a little quiet lately, but she's working such long hours. I think I'd know if she'd started back again."

Blanche returned from the kitchen holding a piece of paper and slowly handed it to Cheryl. "This was on the floor under the table. The cat must've knocked it off the counter."

Blanche watched Cheryl's expression change as she read. A lock of brown, shoulder-length hair fell in Cheryl's face; she tossed it back in place easily with a flick of her wrist. Her light brown eyes widened as she continued reading Mickey's cramped, sloppy script. Blanche's heart had finally stopped tap dancing with worry for her daughter, but it had begun a new, dreadfully different aching for the woman in front of her.

I'm in Mexico with my new lover. I'll be back in a week. We'll talk then.

Mickey

Blanche expected more tears, hysteria, screaming. Almost anything other than total silence. The shock on Cheryl's face and the devastation in her eyes pierced Blanche's heart.

"I'm so sorry, baby," Blanche said. Her voice trembled as she spoke. She took Cheryl in her arms

4

and vowed to shake the living shit out of Mickey the next time she saw her.

"She's *what?*" Phoebe snapped after scanning the note. "Is she out of her mind?"

"This isn't the time, darling," Blanche whispered to her lover.

"We raised her better than this!"

"Please, Phoebe. Not now."

"I'm sorry I got you out of bed for nothing," Cheryl said in a monotone.

Blanche hugged her again, more for herself than for Cheryl. How could Mickey do such a thing to this wonderful person? Cheryl was so good for Mickey. She had helped her through a nasty bout with the bottle last year and had put a roof over their heads and clothes on their backs while Mickey went to law school. Cheryl was so nurturing and sane! Blanche couldn't imagine anyone being more right for her daughter. How could Mickey do this?

"I need to be alone right now," Cheryl whispered.

"I'm not sure that's a good idea just yet," Blanche said. There were questions Blanche wanted to ask and things she wanted to say. Questions, like *How could you not know that Mickey was fooling around? She's so damned obvious when she's bad!* And the things she wanted to say, like *Yes, my Mickey's a shit, but she loves you, Cheryl. I know she loves you.*

"Please," Cheryl said, her voice faltering slightly. "This is so humiliating." She was up from the sofa and striding toward the door. Once it was open, she leaned against it and waited for them to get their things together.

"I don't like this," Phoebe whispered.

5

"Maybe you should go on home without me," Blanche said to her lover. "I'll stay here and talk to her for a while."

"No," Cheryl said. "Please. Both of you just go. I can't see anyone right now."

They reluctantly made their way to the door where they hugged her fiercely. During the ride home and on into the next day, Blanche recalled the sound of Cheryl crying after she had closed the door. Mickey was in seriously big trouble this time. Seriously big trouble.

Blanche answered the door the following afternoon and broke into a radiant smile.

"My daughter the doctor," she said, giving Elaine a hug.

"Your message sounded important," Elaine said. "What's up? Is anybody sick? Is Phoebe okay?"

"It's a long story." Blanche slipped her arm around Elaine's waist and strolled to the kitchen where Phoebe was grating carrots.

"Hey, stranger," Phoebe said. "How's the skin business these days?"

"I've had a rash of patients lately."

Eyes rolled, followed by groans. Elaine was a dermatologist enjoying her second year in private practice. She and Phoebe always traded the same tired dermatology one-liners whenever they saw each other.

Elaine gazed over Phoebe's shoulder at the bowl she was slowly filling with shredded carrots. "Carrots are good for you. Why are you grating them?"

"I'm making a cake," Phoebe said. "Can you stay for dinner? Your mother made soup today." She nodded toward the oven. "And the cornbread's almost ready."

Blanche opened the oven and peeked in. "When did you talk to your sister last?" Blanche asked.

"Your birthday a few weeks ago." Elaine pulled out a stool from the counter. "Why?"

"She ran off to Mexico with some floozy, that's why."

"Cheryl's not a floozy," Elaine said sharply. Phoebe's carrot stopped in mid-stroke against the grater. The oven door remained propped open a tad as Blanche turned to look at her.

"Who said anything about Cheryl?" Blanche roared. "Mickey's got a new lover. Did you know anything about this?"

After a moment Phoebe reached over and tapped the bottom of Elaine's chin to help close her mouth.

"Uh . . . no," Elaine said finally. Phoebe handed her the rest of a carrot to nibble on.

"Are you sure Mickey didn't say anything to you?" Blanche said.

"Mickey and I aren't close anymore. You know that." Elaine took a vicious bite of the carrot nub. "Damn! Lawyers are such *ass*holes!"

Phoebe and Blanche both burst out laughing. Having been raised by two nurses, Elaine and Mickey had spent most of their childhood hearing their mother and her lover discuss the shortcomings of almost every doctor they knew or had to work with. The phrase *doctors are such assholes* never failed to enter a description of how one's day went at the hospital. But once Elaine had been accepted to

7

medical school, the phrase was not uttered again in her presence. Elaine did, however, enjoy getting a good shot in on lawyers — her sister's chosen profession — every chance she got.

As Blanche ladled out bowls of homemade soup, Phoebe leaned over to Elaine and whispered, "Let Mickey and Cheryl work this out."

Elaine gave her a curious look.

"I mean it," Phoebe said.

"Okay, okay."

"What are you two mumbling about?" Blanche asked. She plopped the cornbread out of the pan and rubbed her hands together. "Let's eat."

Cheryl Trinidad turned the pages of yesterday's paper, scanning articles with a fresh Kleenex in her hand. Filtering out the noise in the library was as natural to her as breathing. She dabbed at another tear that rolled down her cheek and felt certain that if one more person asked her what was wrong she'd probably explode.

Had it only been two days since Blanche had found the note? That short, devastating, three-sentence-poor-excuse note. When Mickey hadn't come home from work by ten o'clock Tuesday night, Cheryl had begun to worry. And how silly *that* had been. How could Mickey just leave this way? For her to arrange for time off at the office took a considerable amount of shuffling of everyone's caseload. Vacations took months to plan for in the DA's office. *How long has she been working on this sin trip?* Cheryl wondered.

She turned the page of the newspaper and tried not to think about the day before. Cheryl had called Mickey's office yesterday morning and been told by her secretary that Mickey was on vacation for a week. For some strange reason, hearing it from this woman made everything even more final than reading Mickey's note.

Cheryl called in sick at the library Wednesday morning and spent the day going from room to room in her house. She was still in shock. She cried occasionally and had trouble thinking clearly. The whole thing seemed so unreal. She couldn't imagine what had happened to their relationship and why Mickey would leave her. The sadness was overwhelming. How could Mickey be so unhappy and Cheryl not know it? And when did she have time to see someone else? *I'm in Mexico with my new lover,* the note had said. Cheryl had chosen not to dwell on that particular line until today. She and Mickey had made love on Sunday; they'd watched a movie in bed and had eaten cold pizza for breakfast. They'd wallowed around naked and happy for hours, so what could have possibly happened between Sunday and Tuesday? The whole thing didn't make any sense.

Cheryl had been a bit dazed as she got ready for work Thursday morning. She almost didn't recognize herself in the mirror with her puffy eyes and red nose. She moved around as if by remote control, barely remembering getting in her car and driving to work. *And when was the last time I ate anything?*

she chastised herself. *Maybe that's why my stomach is staying so queasy.*

"How long have you worked at this branch?" a curt voice asked, interrupting her thoughts.

Cheryl looked up from the newspaper and blinked Janet Landro into focus in front of her desk.

"About a month. What are you doing here?"

Janet tossed her bangs away from her eyes. "We need to talk," she said, lowering her voice. "Our lovers are in Cancun fucking their brains out. Can we get some privacy around here?"

Cheryl slowly folded the paper and set it aside. *Veronica? Mickey's in Cancun with Veronica? Her new lover is someone I know?* Cheryl felt light-headed for a moment. She took a series of deep breaths and shuddered.

"There's an office in the back," she managed to say. How was it possible to feel any more numb than she already felt?

She led the way through the tiny tables and chairs in the juvenile section. Someone was reading to a group of children in the corner.

"Did Mickey leave a note?" Janet asked once the office door was closed.

Cheryl cleared her throat. "Yes."

"Was it as descriptive as mine? And the bitch emptied our checking account. I can't even make the house payment."

Cheryl stood by the desk with her arms crossed over her chest. The tears were gone now, but something even more disturbing seemed to be happening to her. "What exactly did Veronica's note say?" She wanted details. Evidence. Times. Places. *Our lovers are in Cancun fucking their brains out.*

"And you wanna know the real pisser with all this?" Janet said. "She bought the Cancun tickets for my *birthday*! We were all set to go!"

Like the usual library noises, Cheryl ignored this outburst and continued to stand there with her arms crossed. "What did Veronica's note say?"

One of Janet's long, slender fingers popped up as she began counting the events off. "They've been seeing each other for about two months, mostly in Mickey's office. Two," she said, popping another finger up, "they're in love and plan on getting a place together when they get back. Three," she said, waving her fingers in Cheryl's face, "the bitch thanked me for loaning her my birthday present! Can you believe that?"

Cheryl slumped against the corner of the desk. Veronica and Mickey worked together. Janet and Veronica had been over to their house several times for dinner in the last few months. They were friends. The four of them were *friends*!

"Thanks for telling me," Cheryl said. She brushed past her and was on her way up front to let someone know she was leaving for the day.

Mickey's in Cancun with Veronica. They've been seeing each other for months. The truth was no longer a jolt, and hearing it from Mickey personally wasn't important anymore. Those fleeting moments of inadequacy that had plagued Cheryl the night before were gone now as well, and the silent promises to win Mickey back didn't apply any longer either.

There's something pathetic about a person who would want someone back after she's treated me this way, Cheryl thought. And she had no desire to be whiny and pathetic any longer. If Mickey Marcaluso wanted out, then fine. She's out forever.

Cheryl grabbed her purse from a desk drawer and left the library with as much dignity and grace as she could muster. Had there been anything in her stomach she might have needed to throw up again, but that wasn't the case now. No, ma'am. That wasn't the case at all now.

Chapter Two

Elaine set her tray on a table in the corner of the hospital cafeteria. She waved at Maxine, who looked a little tired already. Elaine smiled as she pulled her chair out. Some of her most memorable moments had been spent here as a child. Phoebe would pick up Mickey and her from school so the three of them could have dinner with Blanche in this very cafeteria. And even while she was still in college, Elaine had shared as many meals as possible with Phoebe here back then.

Elaine felt as close to Phoebe Carson as she did

her own mother. Phoebe and Blanche had been lovers for twenty-five years, and Phoebe had done her share of carpooling and baking just like the other mothers on the block. Phoebe knew Elaine and Mickey so well that at times it was almost scary. *And she's got me pegged with this Cheryl thing too*, Elaine thought wearily.

Elaine emptied her tray and set it on another table close by. Her salad looked fresh, which was a pleasant surprise considering what time it was. Maxine had gotten called away for an emergency cesarean earlier, but a late lunch had worked out better for both of them anyway.

"You're looking a bit ragged today, Dr. Weston," Elaine said with a smirk.

"I should, Dr. Marcaluso." Maxine sat down and slowly emptied her tray of a chicken salad sandwich and coffee.

"Which is it?" Elaine asked. "The early surgery this morning or that nymphomaniac you're dating?"

Maxine chuckled and shook her head. "She insisted on driving me to work this morning. We're stuck in the usual traffic, creeping along I-10, when she reaches over and —"

"Is this another sex-on-the-interstate story?"

"No," Maxine said simply. "This is a creative-foreplay story. We didn't have sex until she parked the car in the patient loading zone out in front of the hospital."

Elaine rolled her eyes. "Jesus."

"*Jesus* is right, honey. And after last night, who would've thought I'd even be able to *walk* today! Holy moly."

"I'm sure I'm not interested in hearing any of this."

Maxine took a few bites of her sandwich and dabbed at her mouth with a napkin. "I don't know what's bothering me more about this relationship. Is it the fact that she dreams up these outrageous things to do, or is it the fact that I'm so willing to do them *with* her? Which is it?"

"You seem to like her a lot."

Maxine threw her head back and laughed. "You've noticed."

"Yeah, I've noticed. I guess I'll need to set bail money aside for that one phone call you'll be allowed after they arrest your young self on some sort of sexual misconduct charge."

Maxine sipped her coffee and then started on the other half of her sandwich. "What a true friend you are. So what's new with you? It's been a while since you've admitted a patient."

"Three this month. You would've known that, but every time I've been here, you've been too busy."

"Are you okay?" Maxine asked, suddenly serious. "You seem a little down."

"I'm fine. Never better." She leaned back in her chair and toyed with her fork. "Mickey and Cheryl broke up. I guess I'm sort of at loose ends."

"Please don't tell me you're still hung up on her, Elaine. Torch-toting doesn't become you." When

15

Elaine didn't say anything, Maxine sighed dramatically and tapped her fingertips on the table. "Cheryl made her choice a long time ago. Forget about her." "She never knew she had a choice," Elaine shot back. "Bullshit! Weren't you seeing her when Mickey entered the picture?" "Yes and no." "Yes and no, my butt. Listen to me," Maxine said urgently. "Forget Cheryl. She's bad news for you. I don't care if Mickey moves out and takes up with a harem of lesbians; Cheryl Trinidad will always be hopelessly in love with her no matter *what* Mickey does. Do you hear me?" "She's not some doormat, Maxine." "She is where your sister's concerned." "I disagree." Elaine got up and threw away their napkins and plastic utensils. Her appetite was suddenly gone. "A harem of lesbians," she mumbled. "Since when did you become a member of the Mickey Marcaluso Fan Club? She's a screwup and a heartbreaker." "Not to mention being a fucking genius in the sack," Maxine said as she finished her sandwich. "You're right," Elaine snapped. "Let's not mention that." She'd forgotten about Mickey and Maxine having had a little fling several years ago. *Yes, indeed. Let's not mention that,* Elaine thought again irritably. In the hallway they looked at each other and shuffled around uncomfortably for a moment. "Good-bye, Dr. Weston," Elaine said finally. "Why I call on you when I need an encouraging word is a complete mystery to me." Maxine laughed. "Until next time."

* * * * *

It was there on the answering machine when Cheryl Trinidad got home from work — Mickey's voice asking for a convenient time when she could drop by and get her things. Mickey and Veronica had been back for three days already. Cheryl didn't waste any time wondering where the new lovers were staying or what they were wearing to work these days. Cheryl and Janet, the newly dumped lovers, had custody of a very large portion of Mickey's and Veronica's professional wardrobes.

Janet Landro had chosen to pitch all of Veronica's belongings out in the front yard for the world to see and choose from. Cheryl, on the other hand, shied away from such a circus-atmosphere display of their breakup. Yes, she would decide what Mickey could and could not have. Cheryl had packed it all in boxes for her already, but she refused to lower herself to Mickey's level. Cheryl didn't want to see her or talk to her right now — the pain and humiliation ran too deep and were still too fresh. Cheryl hurt in a way she didn't understand yet. Where there should've been bitterness and devastation, she found only disappointment and a vague sense of loss. Cheryl believed that she was still in shock about all of this and didn't like the emptiness that seemed to overwhelm her. She couldn't cry any more, and her anger had moved into another phase. But those old feelings of inadequacy were returning; the old wounds had been torn open. Wounds from being shuffled from foster home to foster home as a child, never really belonging anywhere until the Trinidads had adopted her, never really feeling wanted until then. It hadn't been easy growing up knowing that your real parents didn't care what happened to you, and Mickey's betrayal had brought those feelings to the surface again. It was that more than the betrayal itself that had hurt Cheryl the most. Mickey's lying and cheating was just a small part of what was happening to her.

She didn't return Mickey's phone calls, the last two of which had been laced with colorful profanity. Cheryl had, however, changed the locks on the doors and reprogrammed her garage door opener to prevent any unwanted surprises. She called Blanche and Phoebe to see if they'd be willing to pick up Mickey's things at their convenience. She also told them how much she wanted to remain a part of their lives.

"This is *it*?" Mickey said. "This is all she gave you?" She rummaged through the last box and sat back on her heels. "What about the CD player? And where's my fountain pen collection?"

"Make a list," Blanche said. She hated being the go-between for feuding ex-lovers. It certainly wasn't her idea of a good time. And to make matters worse, Blanche found herself having to fight to stay neutral. Siding with Cheryl didn't seem like the motherly thing to do, since Mickey was her daughter, but voicing her displeasure over the way Mickey was handling this didn't really seem very neutral either. Blanche bit her tongue and grumbled a lot, but the bottom line remained the same — it was Mickey's life, and interfering in it would make her act no better.

"Didn't you give Cheryl that CD player for Christmas last year?" Phoebe asked.

"I paid for it," Mickey said, "so I consider it mine." She picked up the huge box and stacked it beside the others. "I've left messages about wanting to pack my own stuff, but she wouldn't call me back. Now she's changed the locks on the doors and got an unlisted phone number. This isn't fair. I won't know what's not here until I *need* it, for crissakes."

Phoebe gave Blanche a nod, which sent her off to the kitchen. This was their prearranged signal for Blanche to find something else to do while Phoebe pumped Mickey for information on the hows and whys of it all. Mickey had always been a bit temperamental and spoiled, but deep down Phoebe and Blanche knew that Mickey would always need more than anyone could possibly give her. There was a serious potential for self-destruction in her makeup, no matter how tough and distant Mickey tried to be. Phoebe's job now was to get some insight into where her head was at the moment.

"How was Cancun?" Phoebe asked.

"Great," Mickey said with an engaging smile. She had her father's good looks and his athletic build. On the surface Mickey had a magnetic personality and could charm the uncharmable, very much like her father, but there was a dark side to Mickey that showed itself occasionally. Phoebe didn't like the Mickey she was having to deal with now.

Phoebe nodded and sat on the sofa across from her. Mickey absentmindedly ran a hand through her black hair. Mickey was very attractive and had just enough butch in her to make her a good lawyer with that in-your-face abruptness and ability to argue a point. *Why do we worry about her so much?* Phoebe wondered. *She's always landed on her feet.*

"Are you and Veronica looking for a place?" Phoebe asked.

"We found an apartment yesterday."

"I see." Phoebe waited for her to elaborate, but nothing else seemed to be forthcoming. "So tell me, what happened with Cheryl? This thing with Veronica came about pretty fast, didn't it?"

Mickey groaned and looked away from her. Phoebe knew by the expression on her face that she was embarrassed and didn't want to talk about it, but Phoebe believed that they deserved a few answers. Cheryl had been an important part of the family, and Mickey had managed to take that away from them practically overnight.

"What happened?" Phoebe asked again.

"She's just not enough for me anymore."

"Not enough how?"

"You know." Mickey squirmed appropriately and jutted her dimpled chin out. "Sexually. Intellectually. It's a lot of things."

"Intellectually?" Phoebe said with a raised eyebrow. The sexual part she didn't care to get into, but this intellectual stuff was another story. *Who the hell is she kidding here?* "Cheryl's a librarian and an archivist," Phoebe said. "Storing and retrieving information is what she does for a living. The woman can carry on an intelligent conversation about any subject you give her."

"She checks out *books*, for crissakes."

"Is that all you think she does?"

"Sure. And it's boring as hell."

Phoebe put her hands up to ward off another outburst. "Okay, okay. Take it easy."

"Look, maybe I handled this badly," Mickey conceded, "but I couldn't tell her about Veronica, okay? I just couldn't tell her. This was easier for me."

Phoebe nodded and tried to get Mickey to look at her, but Mickey wasn't cooperating.

"Your mother and I intend to keep up with Cheryl. She's a part of our lives, and we care about her."

"What about Veronica?" Mickey said. "She deserves that place now."

"Your partners are always welcome in this house. You know that. But the rest might take some time."

Mickey sighed. "Why does everything have to be so fucking complicated?"

"Because you've made it that way, Mickey. There's a reason taking the easy way out never works."

"I don't need a lecture." She got up and tucked in a flap on a box. "I need my CD player and my fountain pen collection."

Cheryl peeped through the drapes to see who was at the door. Janet stood there with a bottle of wine in hand.

"You changed your phone number," Janet said. "Is Mickey still calling you?"

"Not anymore." Cheryl smiled as she watched Janet make herself comfortable on the sofa and pull a corkscrew from her jacket pocket. "Do you always carry a corkscrew with you?"

"I wasn't sure you'd have one here," Janet said sheepishly.

"Is it safe to assume you have a glass in the other pocket, or should I get you one?"

Janet's go-to-hell look made them both laugh. Cheryl returned moments later with a wineglass for her.

"You aren't joining me?"

"I wasn't invited," Cheryl said. She marked her place in her book and set it on the coffee table. "But no thanks anyway."

"I've never seen you drink before," Janet said. "I thought it was because of Mickey."

They both felt the tension in the air at the mention of Mickey's name. Mickey's problem with alcohol wasn't a secret, but it was something no one really talked about.

"Tell me how you're doing," Cheryl said. "Is it getting any easier?"

Janet stretched her legs out and ran her fingers through her short, brown hair. As she drank her wine, she began talking about Veronica and the plans they'd made together. She cried and cursed a bit, and told Cheryl intimate details of their life together. Janet was so absorbed in herself and her own problems that she didn't notice how uncomfortable all of this was making Cheryl. The more Janet drank and carried on, the better she seemed to get — as if sitting on Cheryl's sofa pouring her heart out was the most healing, therapeutic thing in the world. Cheryl could almost picture the woman leaving there totally cured. *Then why can't I talk about it?* Cheryl wondered. *Is it all festering inside ready to blow at any moment?*

"I'm messed up," Janet mumbled a while later. The bottle was empty, and her voice had lost its projecting power. She was tired of talking and was very close to falling asleep. Cheryl helped her stretch out and took her shoes off. She covered Janet with a blanket and went to bed. Changing her phone number had been easy, but how does one do the same for an address without moving?

Phoebe called Cheryl at work the following day to ask if she'd like to come over for dinner.

"Please," Phoebe said. "We miss you. Blanche and I are both off."

"I don't know," Cheryl said. "I'm not very good company right now." *And what if Mickey should drop by while I'm there?* she thought. The prospect of seeing Mickey again depressed her. She wasn't ready for that yet, and being at Blanche and Phoebe's house for any length of time was surely courting disaster.

"Then how about dinner somewhere?" Phoebe suggested. "There's a new Mexican restaurant on the Saint Mary's strip. We had lunch there the other day."

Cheryl reluctantly agreed. She tried not to think about the last time that she had seen them — that awkward afternoon when she helped Blanche and Phoebe load up Mickey's things. Cheryl hadn't cried since those first few days after Mickey left. She knew what was happening to her, but she didn't know what to do about it.

As a child, she had cried the first few times she had been placed in a new foster home. Each move seemed to harden her a little more and make her withdraw from things. After a while she didn't let anyone see how much she was hurting. That was about the time she had discovered books and how easy it was to escape into the world of fiction.

After the Trinidads adopted her, things became easier. Cheryl lost herself in fiction where good triumphed over evil. She lost herself in trying to learn all there was to know about everything. From school she went every day to the library where she stayed until closing time. On Saturdays she was the first one there and the last one to leave. She became a model student and remained a shy, pensive teenager until a drunk driver took her new parents away. She cried for them once and, until Mickey, nothing in her life had been important enough to make her cry again. Mickey had tapped into that hidden place Cheryl had long ago forgotten. Cheryl had let Mickey in, and she now regretted having done so. Mickey had abused that privilege more than once, and now the tears were all gone.

Cheryl hugged Blanche and Phoebe before she sat down at their table. Blanche looked tired, but her brown eyes seemed to twinkle as she smiled at her. A mop of black hair with generous streaks of gray through it covered Blanche's head. She was a little taller than Cheryl, a good five-seven, and was thin compared to her lover. Phoebe, on the other hand, was closer to Cheryl's height and carried about twenty extra pounds on her medium frame. Phoebe had dull blondish hair mixed with gray. She wore it in a short, wake-up-and-shake shag. Neither of them looked old enough to retire yet, but lately that was all they could talk about.

The three of them looked at their menus and asked questions of the waiter. After they ordered, Cheryl reached down and handed over a plastic bag.

"Let's get the unpleasantness out of the way first," Cheryl said. "I received a nasty little note from Mickey about the CD player and her pen collection."

Blushing, Blanche said, "She's been after us to talk to you."

"But that's *not* why we asked you to dinner," Phoebe said, irritated.

"I know that." Cheryl nudged the plastic bag in Blanche's direction. "This is her fountain pen collection, but I have a problem with giving back the CD player. If Mickey insists that I return my Christmas present, then I'll have to ask her to return her law books. I paid for them while she was going to school. I love *all* books — even books I'll never read or use. That's the deal."

Phoebe's burst of laughter turned heads all around the restaurant.

"She won't like that suggestion," Blanche said with a chuckle.

Cheryl nodded and shrugged. "Then tell her to sue me."

Chapter Three

Elaine had been designated the official note taker, but Maxine still had a pen and tablet in front of her, along with a stack of pamphlets and a few books. They had agreed to do a workshop on women's health for the Texas Lesbian Conference in San Antonio next month. The deadline for summarizing their workshop and sending in a proposal of what they planned to present was quickly approaching, and neither could put it off any longer.

"You cover the menopause portion, and I'll do the

nutrition," Elaine said. "We've got some good material here for handouts. I'll have my secretary call tomorrow and order extra copies of these three in particular." They both scribbled a few notes.

"I'll need about twenty minutes on the pros and cons of artificial hormone replacement," Maxine said, "and we never have enough time for a good question-and-answer session."

Elaine picked up another pamphlet. "Then maybe we should skip nutrition altogether or just touch on it a little. You could easily do an hour on drugs and menopause and have them begging for more." Elaine looked at her as she thumbed through the pamphlet. "I could be your assistant, I guess. Pass out brochures, dim the lights for your slide presentation, make sure the pointer's extended properly."

"I'm not doing this thing alone," Maxine said. "Each workshop needs two presenters, so don't try to weasel out of this."

Thirty minutes later they had an outline completed and the form for their proposal filled out. Either one of them could conduct this workshop in her sleep right now if she had to.

"So," Maxine said as she gathered up her papers and began stuffing them in her briefcase. "What's the latest on the Cheryl-and-Mickey soap opera?"

"Mickey's definitely living with someone else, and no one's heard much from Cheryl." Elaine jotted down the titles of a few pamphlets before Maxine swept them away. "I've been thinking about dropping by to see her."

"Bad idea," Maxine said. "The next thing you know you'll be wanting to ask her out."

"I *do* want to ask her out."

"See what I mean?" Maxine said. "Stay away from her, Dr. Marcaluso. She'll be back in Mickey's bed within a month. Mark my words. This isn't over for them. Save yourself some heartache." Maxine stopped gathering and sorting papers and glanced over at her. "Oh, Jesus, Elaine. You're not still in love with her, are you?"

Elaine didn't say anything; she couldn't look at Maxine right then.

"Oh, hell," Maxine said, her tone much softer now, "if she's that important to you, then do what you have to do." On her way to the door Maxine hugged her. "Maybe you should talk to Phoebe. She's great at this sort of thing."

"I'll think about it." Elaine closed the door and leaned against it. *Phoebe's already warned you to stay out of it*, she thought wearily. *You'll get no help from that one.*

A stroke of luck finally rolled Elaine's way a few days later. Her mother had called her at the office to see if Elaine could donate a few hours on Saturday to the free clinic. Blanche ran the schedule for the clinic. Everything had been covered until one doctor was called out of town with a death in the family. As Elaine and her mother were talking about the clinic's schedule, Blanche mentioned that she and Phoebe were meeting Cheryl for dinner again that night. With a few cleverly phrased questions, Elaine knew where they would be and when they'd be there. A whole scenario played itself out in her head as they talked — Elaine envisioned herself being at the restaurant at the same time, hoping to be invited to join them; Elaine possibly getting there early and already having a table where the three of them could join *her* instead; hanging out in the restaurant parking lot; possibly whizzing by their table to say a few words. *This is nuts, Marcaluso. You don't need an excuse to see this woman! It's a free country!*

"Mom, I need a favor," Elaine said quickly. Blanche stopped chattering about this year's pecan crop in mid-sentence. "I'll work the next two Saturdays at the clinic if you'll do me this one little favor."

"*Two* Saturdays?" Blanche said incredulously.

"Yes. Two Saturdays."

"Goodness. Let me get my calendar out. Two Saturdays? What kind of favor is this? One of those watch-my-cat-for-a-week favors? You know Phoebe's allergies can't stand a cat for more than a few hours at a time."

"Nothing like that," Elaine assured her. "All I'd like you to do is invite me over to dinner this week and have Cheryl there too."

"You and Cheryl over for dinner? That's it?" Blanche didn't even attempt to hide the surprise in her voice.

"That's it." Elaine let out the deep breath she'd been holding. *This even* smells *like a setup, Marcaluso. How embarrassing! You're asking your mother to set you up with your sister's ex-lover!*

"Cheryl isn't too crazy about spending time over here these days," Blanche said.

Elaine rubbed the bridge of her nose and

instantly regretted having said anything. *What a stupid idea, Marcaluso. Phoebe will be all over you for this!*

"Maybe if I invite a few other people over too it won't be so bad for her," Blanche said. "We've been meaning to have a little something anyway. And I can call Mickey and make sure she won't show up by accident."

More people, Elaine thought. *Jesus. Now my setup has been turned into a dinner party.*

"Let me work on this and get back to you," Blanche said. "In the meantime, don't make any plans for the next two Saturdays."

Elaine parked in front of Blanche and Phoebe's house and checked her reflection in the rearview mirror one more time. Cheryl's car was there along with three others Elaine didn't recognize. She'd spent an hour getting dressed, and her bedroom was a mass of clean clothes and empty hangers strung everywhere.

"My daughter the doctor," Blanche said as she opened the door. Everyone in the living room laughed and greeted her with either a hug or a wave.

Elaine nodded at Cheryl and felt her heart do a little tango. *Mickey must be out of her mind,* she thought. *Absolutely out of her mind.*

Cheryl wore a light denim dress with short sleeves and a full, flaring skirt that hit her at mid-calf. Her brown boots came to just below the knee and matched the copper buttons on the dress as well as the small buckle on the belt. *Mickey is absolutely and positively out of her mind*, Elaine mused as she tried to force herself to keep from staring.

Cheryl's light brown hair fell past her shoulders in a cloud of riveting layers. She was beautiful, and Elaine wasn't sure if she could get through this evening without making a complete, drooling fool of herself. She showed a bit of restraint by not rushing across the room and joining in on Cheryl's conversation with Phoebe right away. Elaine managed to mingle a bit before ending up over there.

"We were just talking about you," Phoebe said. She put her arm around Elaine's shoulder and brought her in closer. "Cheryl was asking about your work at the state hospital."

And with that, Elaine was delighted to have Cheryl's undivided attention for the next hour. They settled on the sofa and sipped the lemonade Phoebe brought them. Cheryl knew about the U.S. Public Health Service Hospital in Carville, Louisiana, where Elaine spent at least two weeks every summer tending to patients with Hansen's disease. Cheryl's compassion for those rejected, maimed, and disfigured people rivaled Elaine's own.

"Carville's the only home some of those people have ever known," Elaine said. "Their families are ashamed of them. They've been disowned and forgotten for years. One woman's father took her there when she was fourteen, left her on the front steps. She's been there for thirty years and hasn't had one single visitor the entire time."

Cheryl reached over and squeezed Elaine's hand. "That's such a sad story," she said. "Are you able to help any of those people?"

Elaine lost her voice for a moment. At first she

wasn't sure if it was because Cheryl had actually *touched* her or because Elaine had just realized that she'd been discussing homeless and abandoned people with someone who had spent the majority of her childhood in foster care.

"Your mother's very proud of you," Cheryl said.

Elaine blushed and cleared her throat. When had Cheryl taken her hand away? How could she have missed that? "I'm proud of her too," Elaine said. "I'm sure it wasn't easy having no education, two toddlers, and a jerk for a husband before she was twenty-one."

Cheryl smiled and draped an arm along the edge of the sofa. "What was it like being raised by two lesbians? It sounds like a dream come true."

"We had our moments," Elaine said with a laugh. "There came a time when there were four cases of PMS to deal with during the course of a month, but it was basically a very normal household."

"When did you know you were gay?" Cheryl asked. Her lips were full and glossy, so kissable that Elaine felt woozy for a moment.

"All suspicions were confirmed my freshman year in college," Elaine said. "A basketball player kissed me under the bleachers one night. Even to this day, really tall women get my pulse to clicking along nicely."

Cheryl's light laughter was refreshing. "Being a part of your family has always meant a lot to me."

"It still should," Elaine said. "You can't divorce feelings. My mother and Phoebe care a lot about you."

"It's mutual. I love them both very much too."

Dinner was a mixture of food trivia and laughter

as eight women tackled a masterpiece of a salad, platters of spaghetti and meatballs, and a garlic bread that made their eyes water. Elaine listened as Cheryl answered a question on the origin of spaghetti and was impressed at how everyone's attention stayed focused on her when Cheryl mentioned a few new health benefits recently associated with garlic.

"So it makes you feel better, but you still smell bad?" Phoebe asked. There was a distinctive, "Oh, shit," which was rapidly followed by howling laughter as Phoebe dabbed at the river of spaghetti sauce oozing down the front of her white shirt.

"Cold water and Spray'n Wash," Cheryl said through arched eyebrows.

More laughter erupted as Phoebe excused herself to change shirts.

Elaine and Cheryl volunteered to clean up the kitchen while Blanche and Phoebe entertained their other guests.

"I'll wash and you dry," Cheryl said. "You should know where everything goes."

Elaine was in heaven. She couldn't have imagined the evening going this well. There'd been no mention of Mickey or the breakup. *Are we all in denial, or is this thing with them really over after all?* Elaine wondered.

"I heard that you and Maxine Weston were doing a workshop at the conference," Cheryl said. "Did the two of you volunteer on your own or did your mother volunteer you?"

"This was our idea," Elaine said. "It's something Maxine and I both support. It's rejuvenating being with five hundred lesbians as they take over a hotel for a weekend."

Cheryl gave her a hot, soapy plate to rinse. "How many of these conferences have you attended? I remember seeing you at the first one held here several years ago."

Elaine laughed as she carefully got all the soapsuds off and then dried the plate. "Don't tell me you were there for the Lesbian Mother/Daughter workshop we did."

"According to the critiques, it ranked right up there with the Leather Dykes in popularity," Cheryl noted.

"That's a compliment if I ever heard one," Elaine said. "Are you on the steering committee this year?"

"I handled all the publicity and news releases, and I'll be selling conference T-shirts." Cheryl smiled shyly as she handed over another plate. "There's no job too small. We still need volunteers for everything."

"Need help peddling those T-shirts?" Elaine asked. Her voice was so calm she'd almost convinced herself that she wasn't nervous. "That sounds easy."

"I'll get your name on the roster before you change your mind."

Change my mind? Fat chance, Elaine thought with a chuckle. Even though the conference was several weeks away still, she wanted to think of the T-shirt vending adventure as a date. *The things you do for love, Marcaluso. You must really have it bad.*

When the kitchen was finally clean, Elaine got them fresh lemonade and suggested they relax on the deck for a few minutes. The sky was clear and filled with stars. Elaine asked about the constellations and listened as Cheryl pointed out and described what was up in the sky that night. Phoebe and Blanche

34

joined them a while later after everyone else had gone home. They pulled up matching lawn chairs.

"The kitchen looks better now than it did when we started this afternoon," Blanche said.

"Everything was wonderful," Cheryl said dreamily.

"And that sauce was such a nice color on that white shirt, Phoebe," Elaine added.

Their laughter melted into an easy lull in the conversation. Cheryl finally broke the comfortable silence by informing them that it was time for her to go. She stated again how much she had enjoyed the evening.

"I found some more things of Mickey's," she said. It was the first time Mickey's name had been mentioned. "I forgot to bring them with me. Let me know when it's convenient, and I'll drop them by."

On impulse, Elaine heard the words pop out of her mouth almost before she was aware of saying them. "I'll be in your neighborhood tomorrow afternoon. Why don't I stop by and pick them up for you?"

"Really?" Cheryl said. "Thanks. That'd be great. Any time after five's good for me."

Elaine's heart was thumping. *Jesus! Now I'll have to cancel that meeting I scheduled tomorrow afternoon.* Her mind raced with details on how she could juggle a few appointments. *Maybe my first date won't be spent over a pile of T-shirts at a conference with five hundred lesbians after all.*

Chapter Four

Elaine pulled into Cheryl's driveway at a few minutes after five and couldn't believe how nervous she felt. All day she'd been dodging Phoebe's phone calls, having no wish to deal with any of that yet, but she had a feeling what the playback on her answering machine would sound like when she got home. She would undoubtedly hear a scathing lecture from Phoebe Carson in the immediate future.

Elaine rang the doorbell and waved at the parted drapes. The door opened to Cheryl's radiant smile.

"Blanche's daughter the doctor," she said, and then laughed easily.

As Elaine came in she noticed the bandage. "What happened to your hand?" It was an impressive wrapping that covered Cheryl's entire left hand, leaving only fingertips exposed.

"Coffee was spilled on me at lunch. It's not as bad as it looks. I kept hitting the burn all afternoon, so I added extra padding." Cheryl led the way through the living room to the kitchen. Elaine couldn't remember the last time she'd been here. *Christmas Eve two years ago maybe,* she thought. The memory depressed her. Cheryl had seemed so happy, even though Elaine had heard rumors then about Mickey sleeping around.

"I'm so glad you're here," Cheryl said. "I've got two favors to ask you, one of which is a bit embarrassing, I'm afraid." She opened the refrigerator and peeked in. "Would you like something to drink? There's a nice assortment here."

"Sure." Elaine opened their diet sodas and smiled. She was both surprised and relieved that her nervousness was gone. "And the two favors are?"

"Oh, yes," Cheryl said. "Favor number one is Cardigan's dinner. I can't seem to operate the can opener with only one hand." She picked up a small can of salmon and indicated one of two electric can openers on the counter. "He gets cranky if I don't feed him as soon as I get home. He never eats right away, of course, but I'm in trouble if I don't at least make the effort to accommodate."

Elaine remembered Cardigan fondly. A stray kitten abandoned in the park two summers ago, chocolate in color and now the size of a small, healthy pig.

"Goodness! Look at you." Elaine bent down to rub behind his ears and was rewarded with a purring marathon. "How about some dinner?" she asked him. Elaine opened the can of salmon and found Cardigan's dish and water bowl near the back door. Cheryl left the kitchen and returned with a medium-sized box balanced on one hand and neatly tucked against her body. She set it down on the counter with a thud and stood staring at it. After a moment she turned around and attempted a tired smile.

"I'm sure you have other things to do," Cheryl said. "I really appreciate this."

"I'm glad I could help." Elaine nodded toward the box. "Are those Mickey's things?"

"Yes." Cheryl sighed heavily. Her entire mood had changed. Elaine saw the weariness in her eyes and heard a strained attempt at normality in her voice. "I'm sure I'll find more as time drags on."

They stood in silence sipping their sodas. Finally Cheryl reached over and unplugged one of the can openers and slowly wrapped the short cord around it.

"This is the one we always had to use for people food," Cheryl said, indicating the can opener. "Cat food and *only* cat food had to be opened with the other one." She looked up and met Elaine's amused yet puzzled expression. "Have you ever heard of anything so asinine and petty in your life? One can opener for people food and one for cat food. Was she like that as a child?"

"Asinine and petty?" Elaine said. "Yes, as a matter of fact she was, but we only had one can opener in the house."

"But no cats or dogs, right? Nothing that would require its own can opener."

"Birds and fish and turtles," Elaine confirmed. She watched as Cheryl took the people food can opener and stuffed it in the box with the rest of Mickey's things. The contents of the box consisted of three paperbacks, a T-shirt, and several cassettes. Cheryl found a roll of tape and let Elaine seal the box for her.

"Are you taking this to your mother's house or giving it directly to Mickey?" Cheryl asked.

"My mother's house."

Cheryl opened a drawer and pulled out a wide, black marker. "Will you turn the box on its side for me please?"

Elaine turned the box over and held it steady for her as Cheryl wrote SEX TOYS in large, perfect letters on all four sides.

"Pretty childish, huh?" she said as she re-emphasized the last batch of letters with the marker. "Your sister's always been able to bring out the worst in me."

"Is this as bad as it gets?" Elaine asked with a laugh. She picked up the box and followed Cheryl out of the kitchen.

"Actually, I'm trying very hard not to hate her." Cheryl leaned against the edge of the front door. "What she did was despicable, but the way she did it was even worse. When someone I love has so little regard for me, it makes me reevaluate my worth as a person. That's the part I'll never be able to forgive her for. She's made me doubt myself again."

"You're the only one who can give her that kind of power," Elaine said.

Cheryl smiled sadly. "You're right, of course, but we're dealing with a mind here. Rational thought hasn't entered the picture yet." Suddenly her expression changed. "I've got something else. I almost forgot." She returned quickly, waving a small certificate in the air. "Along with giving me a free lunch this afternoon," she said indicating her bandaged hand, "the restaurant where coffee was spilled on me also gave me a complimentary dinner for two. I thought about asking my friend Janet to go, but all she can talk about is Mickey and Veronica. It's so depressing being around her. So," Cheryl said as she waved the coupon in the air again, "maybe you can get some use out of this, and if not then maybe Blanche and Phoebe can."

Elaine glanced at the coupon and then at Cheryl. Before she really knew what was happening, her mouth was working again. "I think you and I should go," Elaine said. "Maybe when your hand is better."

"Oh," Cheryl said. "Yes. I suppose we could. Why didn't I think of that? How about tomorrow? Are you free tomorrow?"

"Sure. Tomorrow's fine," Elaine said, her heart racing. "I'll pick you up at six."

Cheryl opened the door for her and then closed it again. "I almost forgot about favor number two," she said. "The embarrassing one." Cheryl turned around with her back to Elaine. "I need two hands to get out of this dress. I can't reach the top button with this bandage on."

Elaine set the box down and willed her hands to stop trembling as she fumbled with the button at the nape of Cheryl's neck. *You're getting to undress her before your first date, Marcaluso. This is a good sign. A real good sign!*

"Thanks," Cheryl said. "You saved me from having to wear the same clothes all week."

"My pleasure. I'll see you tomorrow."

"She's amazing," Maxine said as she punctuated certain words with a three-pronged plastic fork. "I've never been with a multiorgasmic woman before."

"Oh, please," Elaine said with a sigh. She didn't need this.

"And she says she can *teach* me!"

"She's probably faking it, Maxine."

"Bullshit."

"Meg Ryan — *When Harry Met Sally*. Best orgasm I ever heard. Trust me. She's faking it."

"You can fake an audio, Dr. Marcaluso, but you can't fake a body response. I'm telling you this woman's a —"

"Okay, okay," Elaine said. She glanced around to see if anyone in the cafeteria was close enough to hear them. "Whatever. Can we talk about something else?"

"Sure. How's it going with your sister's ex-lover?"

Elaine set her fork down and leaned back in her chair. She blinked several times as the shock settled around her. Maxine must've seen the look on her face because she immediately began apologizing.

"I'm sorry. I shouldn't have said that."

Elaine's appetite, what little appetite she'd had all day, was gone. The night before, she'd been too excited to sleep, and today she hadn't been able to eat anything.

"What is it about Cheryl that makes you dislike her so?" Elaine asked. "Other than the fact she's my sister's ex-lover?"

Maxine snapped the plastic top back on her salad. Neither of them seemed to have much of an appetite.

"All I can see is you getting hurt, Elaine. I can't get beyond that." Maxine absentmindedly spun her fork around on the table. "You're my friend, and I care about you." She shrugged and set the fork on top of the salad box. "Maybe it's time I mind my own business. You're a big girl. You don't need me telling you when you're screwing up."

Elaine laughed bitterly. "You're right. I've got Phoebe for that."

Cheryl answered the door with her usual smile and a smaller bandage on her hand. "My friend the doctor," she said. "Come in. I'm almost ready."

"How's your hand?"

"Better today. Thanks."

At the restaurant they good-naturedly debated over whether or not to have coffee with their meal. Elaine suggested that they both wear mittens if they did. Cheryl had been immediately recognized, and the staff were eager to make their dining experience a pleasant one. They were seated immediately at the best table and were advised which wines and champagnes were available.

"This is nice, but it's still not worth it," Elaine said. "Burns are very painful. They're getting off too easily."

"Then let's make the most of it."

Elaine relayed, in acute detail, how Blanche and Phoebe reacted to the box Elaine had delivered the evening before.

"They were both speechless," Elaine said. "It was great. Phoebe kept shaking the box and picking it up. They had no idea sex toys were so heavy."

Cheryl's laughter was refreshing and delightful, and Elaine wanted to hear more of it.

"Tell me about them," Cheryl said. "I love hearing stories about your family."

"Haven't you heard them all before?" Elaine asked.

"You mean from Mickey? No. She would never talk about anything personal." Cheryl's smile was softened by the candlelight. She met Elaine's eyes across the table. "The two of you are so different. Like night and day."

"I'll certainly take that as a compliment."

"So tell me something about yourself," Cheryl said. "Are you the only doctor in your family?"

"I have a cousin in California who's a rheumatologist. Only a few people in the family really know what he does."

"Are you and Mickey the only lesbians? Besides Blanche, of course."

Elaine smiled. "My Aunt Sophia's in the convent. There's always hope for her." As their salads arrived, Elaine took the opportunity to condense her family tree and twenty-five years of life with Phoebe and Blanche into a few meaningful paragraphs.

"My parents come from good, Italian Catholic stock," Elaine said. "My mother is one of ten children, and my father's one of eight. They were both born and raised in New York. On my father's side we've got two lawyers, a priest, a restaurant owner, a used car salesman, and three homemakers. On my mother's side — the Benedettis — there's a nurse, a gardener, a museum curator, three violinists, a telephone lineman, two homemakers and Aunt Sophia in the convent. Has anyone ever told you what my mother's real name is?"

"No," Cheryl said.

"Bianca Valente Benedetti," Elaine said slowly. "I always thought it was such a beautiful name, especially when my grandmother says it, but my mother prefers being called Blanche." Elaine enjoyed Cheryl's laughter. "My parents have never divorced," Elaine continued. "They'd rather live in sin and pretend no one will notice. I've got about thirty cousins from my father's side and about that many on my mother's, and I try to attend the family reunions when I can."

"Your parents were never divorced?" Cheryl said, the surprise clearly registering on her face.

"No. My mother has this great little speech about the pope and divorce and being a good Catholic lesbian. She gives it whenever she sees my Aunt Sophia. I'll have her recite it for you some time. It's quite entertaining."

"I had no idea."

"Mickey never talked about the Marcalusos and the Benedettis?" Elaine asked. She laughed after a moment. "Keep asking me questions, and I can talk about my family all night." *I do love my family,*

44

Elaine thought. *I like being with them and talking about them. And here sits the woman I love — someone who's never had a real family long enough to feel like she belongs anywhere. I can't make her love me by sharing bits of Marcaluso trivia, but I sure as hell can let her see a side of me that few people know about.*

"How do your parents get along now?" Cheryl asked. "I still can't believe they've never divorced!"

"It was far from pleasant at first, but now my mother, Phoebe, and my father all get along great. They stay with him whenever they visit New York. He has his women, but he has no desire to remarry."

Salads were cleared away and entrées served. Cheryl continued asking an array of questions about everything from growing up Italian to the astronomical cost of medical school, and Elaine answered all questions as best she could. After describing a typical day in the life of a dermatologist, Elaine offered a question of her own.

"What happened with you and Mickey? Can you talk about it?"

Cheryl shrugged and pursed her lips thoughtfully. "I imagine a lot of it was my fault. I expected too much from her. Things like fidelity and honesty. I made the mistake of assuming too much. I take commitment very seriously, and the only thing Mickey has ever taken seriously is her work."

"She's hurt you deeply."

"I'm very angry and embarrassed by this whole chain of events." Cheryl reached for her water glass and met Elaine's gaze in the candlelight. "I have a similar question for you," she said. "Something happened between you and Mickey too. Your mother says you were close at one time."

It's you, Elaine answered silently. *We both fell in love with you.*

"I used to wonder what it would be like to have a sister," Cheryl said. "And to have one who's also lesbian sounds like heaven." She smiled sadly. "I hope Mickey's a better sister than she was a lover."

Elaine laughed and didn't quite know what to say. Cheryl's smile faded after a moment.

"I'm not sure what's happening to me," Cheryl said. "My emotions don't make any sense."

"Are you still in love with her?" Elaine asked. She held her breath waiting for an answer — a yes would be devastating. Elaine wasn't ready to hear an answer, no matter what it was, right then.

"I don't know," Cheryl said. "It stands to reason that I should be. It even worries me that I can't say for sure that I am." She closed her eyes and visibly shivered. "God, I don't want to be."

But it looks like you are, Elaine thought.

"The shock has worn off," Cheryl said, "and I know that my anger is understandable. It's the humiliation that I'm having so much trouble with. Your mother's finding Mickey's note was awful. Phoebe and Blanche didn't know what to say, and I just wanted to be left alone. I felt used and abused, and if I'm still in love with her after all of that, then I need my head examined."

"You can't avoid her forever, you know."

It was Cheryl's turn to laugh. "Sure I can."

Before they knew it, they were the only customers left in the restaurant.

"What time is it?" Elaine asked as she squinted at her watch in the candlelight.

"Ten-thirty," Cheryl said. "That can't be right."

On the way back to Cheryl's house she asked Elaine more questions about her family, and those amusing pearls of wisdom just kept falling from Elaine's lips. It wasn't lost on her that Cheryl had stated twice that she'd had a good time. Things were looking up; Elaine was cautiously optimistic.

Chapter Five

Cheryl was furious when she answered the phone at work a few days later and heard Mickey's voice. Rendered speechless for a moment, even Cheryl herself was surprised at the unprecedented rage that rumbled inside of her.

"How *dare* you call me here!" she seethed.

"What am I supposed to do?" Mickey barked. "I leave messages at the front desk that are never returned, my letters have gone unanswered, and you've changed your goddamned *phone* number! We've got things to discuss."

"I have nothing to say to you." And with that Cheryl slammed the phone down. An hour later, however, Mickey managed to get her back on the line again.

"The property at the lake," Mickey said in a frustrated hurry, but all Cheryl had to do was hear her voice before returning the receiver to its rightful place.

Later that same afternoon Mickey had someone else call. When Cheryl was on the line, Mickey snatched the handset and proceeded with her spiel.

"I want that property, Cheryl. I'm willing to —"

"If you ever call me here again, Mickey, I'll file a complaint against you for harassment." Cheryl's voice was so calm and unnatural sounding that a coworker nearby stopped to look at her. "If you have something to say to me you can either write to me, relay a message through your mother, or contact my lawyer, but don't ever, and I mean *ever*, call me here again. Is that understood?" She hung up once more, feeling confident that Mickey Marcaluso wouldn't be calling her at work again. Cheryl put the tired, sordid incident out of her mind as though it had never happened.

Early Saturday evening Cheryl closed her bedroom door, leaving Cardigan snoozing on the comforter at the foot of the bed. Phoebe would be able to stay longer with the cat somewhere else in the house. Cheryl had invited Blanche, Phoebe, Janet, and Elaine over for dinner. Entertaining and keeping busy always made her feel better.

Blanche and Phoebe arrived first, followed by Janet, whose car had died a block down the road. She was busy on the phone arranging for a tow truck.

"Can I help with anything?" Blanche asked Cheryl in the kitchen. She closed her eyes and took a deep, dreamy breath near a simmering pot. "It smells heavenly in here."

"You can take these in the living room and help Phoebe and Janet eat them." Cheryl slid the hors d'oeuvres from the refrigerator as the doorbell rang. "And if you could answer that, I'd appreciate it."

Blanche opened the front door and gave Elaine a hug. "My daughter the doctor. Come in. Come in. Cheryl's in the kitchen."

Elaine waved at Phoebe, who was comfortable in an overstuffed chair near the fireplace. "Hey, Doc," Phoebe called. "How's the skin business?"

"Adequate but hairy," Elaine answered. "And you?" She peered curiously at Janet, who was on the phone giving someone directions. *How many more people are supposed to be here?* she wondered. Elaine had been looking forward to this all week, even though she knew she wouldn't be alone with Cheryl. She hoped to take care of that later after everyone else had gone, though. At this point just *being* here was a major accomplishment. In the kitchen Elaine found her stirring some sort of cheese sauce and adjusting the heat on a burner.

"Ah," Cheryl said with a warm smile. "You're here."

Elaine laughed and wasn't at all surprised that

the fluttering returned to her stomach. Everything looked so good on this woman, and the colors Cheryl usually wore were always perfect — autumn colors, light oranges and browns, forever bringing out the highlights in her hair. *You're drooling, Marcaluso. You're drooling.*

"Would you like something to drink?" Cheryl asked. "Your mother tells me you volunteered at the clinic today."

Elaine was delighted to have been the subject of a conversation earlier. She had obviously been on Cheryl's mind at least once today.

"My mother was kind enough to schedule me for a ten-minute lunch. Those three Fig Newtons I found in a desk drawer at eleven-thirty wore off hours ago."

Cheryl tilted her head and gave Elaine a slow, interested look. Elaine's pulse quickened as their eyes met.

"Three Fig Newtons?" Cheryl said. "Then I'll see if I can take care of that appetite of yours."

Elaine could feel the heat rising in her face as she nervously cleared her throat.

Janet came into the kitchen grumbling about warranties for new cars. Cheryl introduced Elaine and Janet and promised them that dinner would be ready soon.

"The other dumpee," Cheryl explained after Janet left the kitchen to set the table. "She's so depressed. This Mickey-and-Veronica thing is all she talks about."

"Then let's keep the evening on a lighter note

when possible," Elaine suggested. "Maybe we should play some parlor games. Like charades or Taboo."

"Oh, please," Cheryl said. "We can do this without resorting to any of that, I'm sure."

And the evening went on, a delicious meal was properly swooned over and consumed, and Blanche, Phoebe, and Elaine talked about their experiences in the hospital. Blanche's tales of double shifts on the psych ward were rivaled only by Elaine's description of her first rotation in a VD clinic, which on the surface didn't sound like something one would discuss over dinner but which in actuality was quite entertaining.

Spirits were high as most of a cheesecake disappeared and the second pot of decaf was brewed. The seating arrangement in the living room later, however, finally tipped Elaine off that something different was happening.

Janet had seemed very attentive all through dinner, making sure Elaine had salt, pepper, drink refills, and anything else she could possibly want. Janet laughed at the right times and asked a string of flattering questions. At one point Elaine noticed Cheryl watching them with unguarded amusement, and at the time it was just so nice to have Cheryl's attention that the immediate reason why Elaine was getting it had escaped her. But once they'd retired to the living room, Elaine noticed how Janet rushed to the sofa to sit beside her and then reached over to nudge her knee after some trivial nonsense Elaine had commented on.

"Where's Cardigan?" Phoebe asked. "I'm breathing so well I forgot all about him."

"He's probably on my bed watching TV," Cheryl said.

"Eating bonbons, no doubt," Blanche added. She gave her lover's hand a squeeze. "Glad to see you're holding up okay."

"Has Cheryl ever told you how Cardigan got his name?" Janet asked Elaine. Her arm was draped along the top of the sofa near Elaine's shoulder.

"Something about his shedding enough hair to make a sweater," Elaine said. She glanced again at Cheryl, who still had that amused look on her face. From there they switched gears and all exchanged animal stories, with Phoebe's contribution always ending with a description of how her throat closed up after being around a cat for very long. A while later Blanche yawned and began making noises about leaving. It was eleven o'clock already.

Elaine checked her watch and hoped everyone was finally ready to go. Getting Cheryl alone wasn't as easy as it had seemed earlier when she'd thought of this, but much to Elaine's disappointment, Janet had other plans.

"Could I bother you for a ride home?" Janet asked her. "My car's in the shop."

Elaine did her best to disguise her disappointment, and she noticed that amused expression on Cheryl's face again as their eyes met across the room. Everyone got ready to leave and exchanged hugs and compliments on dinner. Cheryl chuckled and gave Elaine a firm pat on the back.

"You're good for her," Cheryl whispered. "And you said you liked them tall."

"What's going on here?" Elaine stammered in a panicky whisper.

"You two ready?" Phoebe asked as she opened the front door. "We can all walk out together."

Elaine leaned toward Cheryl and whispered, "Expect a phone call from me when I get home." If she stopped to think about this for even a moment, she'd probably get pissed!

"When?" Cheryl teased. "Three or four hours from now? Don't even think about calling me that late."

"Twenty minutes, tops." Elaine didn't know where Janet lived, but she'd get her there and be on her way home in record time. *This is unreal,* she thought. *Totally unreal. Three or four hours? What the hell's that supposed to mean?*

Elaine dropped Janet off at a nice split-level garden home in Castle Hills. It was an expensive neighborhood; Maxine and Betina didn't live that far away. Conversation en route had consisted of Janet's asking more questions about Elaine's practice and Elaine's occasional responses that were often no more than one syllable. They were both a bit distracted when Janet invited her in for a drink, but Elaine's refusal was less awkward than expected. It *was* late, after all.

Four blocks down the road, once she'd dropped Janet off, Elaine reached for her cellular phone and dialed Cheryl's number, but the line was busy. All the way home Elaine kept trying, but she got nothing but a busy signal. *Could Cheryl have taken the phone off the hook?* she wondered. *Even after hearing me say I'd call?* Elaine was so disappointed that she felt like crying. Forty-five minutes later she pulled into her garage and sat in her car for a while, hating her insane bursts of disappointment.

She got out of the car and let herself into her house through the kitchen. As soon as she opened the door she heard a woman's voice talking in the living room. It took her a moment to realize that Cheryl was leaving a message on the answering machine, but by the time Elaine raced to the telephone Cheryl had hung up already. Elaine eased down on the sofa and pushed the play button to listen.

"In case you've been trying to call me," Cheryl's voice said, "I've been on the phone with Janet ever since you took her home. She seemed to be a bit smitten by you. And in case you *haven't* been trying to call, then my question to you is why not? You said twenty minutes. Tops. And it's been forty-five already."

Elaine reached for the phone and took a deep breath. She couldn't remember the last time she had felt this happy. She dialed Cheryl's number and listened as that quiet, husky voice answered.

"Hi," Elaine said. "I just got your message." She wanted to know where Cheryl was right then — curled up on the sofa in front of the TV? In the kitchen cleaning up from the evening's festivities? Elaine couldn't bring herself to ask, though. She preferred imagining Cheryl in bed dressed in a simple nightgown in the middle of a mountain of pillows.

"You've worked magic on Janet's self-esteem,"

Cheryl said. "She talked about you for thirty minutes nonstop."

Elaine wasn't sure how to respond to that. The last thing in the world she wanted to do was give Cheryl an excuse to tease her further.

"Don't you care about what she said?" Cheryl asked.

Elaine laughed. "Not really."

"Oh. Have I misinterpreted the situation?"

Elaine began to relax a little and leaned her head back against the sofa. "What situation might that be?"

"I picked up some serious vibes this evening," Cheryl said. "And Janet's made it clear that she's interested in you."

"Whatever vibes you picked up from me weren't meant for Janet, I can assure you."

There was a moment of silence before Cheryl once again said a simple "Oh."

The lack of a more enthusiastic response caught Elaine's attention. She'd spoken too soon. It was obvious that Cheryl wasn't ready to hear any of this yet.

"Let's leave it at that for now," Elaine said quickly. "I . . . uh . . . was wondering if you'd have dinner with me some time this week. We could go downtown and mingle with the tourists. It's been ages since I did any of that."

There was another extended silence before Cheryl said, "Elaine . . . I had no idea . . ."

"Please," Elaine whispered. "Forget I said anything. Let's forget about the vibes and forget about Janet. How about dinner on Tuesday? We'll be tourists. Do the River Walk and Planet Hollywood or the Hard Rock Cafe. Maybe all three. The works."

"You like that sort of thing?"

"Being a tourist?"

"No. Planet Hollywood. The Hard Rock. All those yuppie places. Please tell me you've never been to Hooters. Please."

Elaine laughed. "I've never been to Hooters."

"Thank you."

"I was raised by two feminists. We couldn't even *say* hooters in our house. So we're on for Tuesday then? I'll pick you up at seven. It'll be fun. I promise."

"I'm sure it will be," Cheryl said. "You've given me a lot to think about. I need to process and reevaluate this whole evening."

"Just keep an open mind. That's all I'm asking for right now."

"Fair enough," Cheryl said. "Then I'll see you Tuesday at seven."

Cheryl's lawyer called to relay Mickey's proposal for the lakefront property that they owned together. Alpha Cooper was tough, and Cheryl had known from the beginning how furious Mickey would be when she found out who was representing her.

"She wants the property but was refusing to pay you for it. Not one red cent," Alpha said in that crisp, dry business tone she could resort to when she was annoyed. "After I stopped laughing and requested that she not waste any more of my time, she reluctantly offered half of the equity you've both already paid in. I'm happy to report that she's now also willing to pay you for half of what the property's worth. We could probably hold out for a bit more. She wants it bad enough. But I wasn't sure how much you wanted to make her squirm."

"Get what you can," Cheryl said quietly. She hated this. The bickering and snipping. She felt heaviness in her chest at the thought of Mickey, but devastation and shock had already been replaced by anger. "Just make sure I don't have to see her."

At work the next day Cheryl spent the morning cataloging and occasionally arguing with the city manager's office over a proposed budget cut. The staff of every public library in town was upset about the rumor. A while later Janet called. Her voice was full of giddy excitement.

"You'll never guess what happened last night," Janet said in a rush. "Veronica came over and we slept together. She had a fight with Mickey. Oh, god it was hot! We've *never* had sex like that before! I'm meeting her again at the house for lunch in an hour. Isn't this great? Lunch. Ha! Food certainly isn't on my agenda today."

Cheryl gripped the telephone so hard that her knuckles were turning white. "Why are you telling me this?"

"Why? Don't you see? Mickey'll come crawling back to you now. This is perfect."

Cheryl was speechless. She didn't want Mickey back, and she didn't want to hear anything about Janet and Veronica either.

"I thought you'd be happy for me," Janet said in a more subdued tone.

This makes you no better than they are, Cheryl wanted to say to her. She leaned back in her chair and rubbed her brow with tense fingertips.

"I'm in love with her, Cheryl. Don't kid yourself. You'd do the same thing if Mickey had shown up on your doorstep."

Cheryl felt a wrenching in the pit of her stomach at just the thought of being that weak and needy. *What would I have done?* she wondered. *Maybe that's why I'm refusing to see her now, why I can't bring myself to even engage in a brief conversation with her. Am I afraid of the hold Mickey has on me? Am I still in love with her? Doesn't it matter that she's left me for a blonde pile of fluff?* Cheryl suddenly felt exhausted. She was tired of thinking and tired of dealing with all these new emotions.

"I'm going for it, Cheryl," Janet said. She'd regained some of her earlier enthusiasm. "Maybe I can convince her to stay all night this time."

"Janet," Cheryl said with a weary sigh. "Veronica went home to Mickey after she left you last night?"

"She said she couldn't stay. I don't know where she went."

"Think about it."

"Christ, Cheryl. Why are you trying to ruin this for me?"

"Will you *listen* to yourself?" Cheryl snapped.

"They ran off to Mexico together. Veronica left you for another woman. Doesn't that mean anything to you?"

"I don't need this right now, okay? I'm sorry I called. I've got a lunch date to get ready for."

Cheryl heard the click in her ear and held the phone in place for a while longer. *I've got more respect for myself than that.* As she hung up, she took a deep breath and rubbed her tired eyes again, praying the whole time that she really *did* have more respect for herself than that.

Chapter Six

Elaine Marcaluso was ready for work early and had a little extra bounce in her step as she moved through her apartment. She'd had a vivid dream about kissing Cheryl, and even now, hours later as she got her briefcase together, she had a tumbling in her stomach whenever she thought about it. She found herself humming silly love songs all the way to the restaurant where she was supposed to meet Maxine for breakfast. She felt great.

In the dream Elaine had picked Cheryl up for dinner, and when they were in the car, it seemed as though Cheryl sat a little closer to her in the seat. Elaine couldn't remember anything they talked about, but she did remember how Cheryl laughed and how her light brown hair framed her lovely face each time she tilted her head. In the dream Elaine had suggested they go to her place after dinner and see the kittens.

"And where in the world did *kittens* come from, Marcaluso?" she asked herself with a chuckle as she wove in and out of traffic. Noah, Elaine's male Persian, didn't have a maternal bone in his body, but in this dream there had been four kittens in a basket just outside of Elaine's laundry room. The kittens were such darling little creatures and barely had their eyes open. The dream had Elaine kneeling on one side of the basket while Cheryl was kneeling on the other. Suddenly their eyes met. They set the kittens down at the same time and leaned toward each other for a kiss. Once the kiss was over, Cheryl got up and turned to walk out of the room, and then Elaine was off dreaming about something else.

"That's it?" Maxine said over her potato-and-egg taco. "Dreaming about a kiss has you in *this* kind of mood? My, my. I wonder what you'd be like if she'd groped you a little."

Elaine tossed a wadded napkin at her.

"What sort of kiss was it?" Maxine asked.

"Good. Jesus, it was good," Elaine said with a sigh. "My stomach was fluttering so much that if I hadn't been asleep already I might've passed out."

Maxine's laughter stopped a few conversations at other tables around them. "Tell me about this kiss," she said, lowering her voice. "Was Cheryl as into it as you were? In the dream, I mean."

"She was definitely kissing me back."

"Why do you think she got up and left the way she did?" Maxine asked.

"I don't know. Maybe she was on her way to my bedroom, hoping I'd follow her."

"Sounds like you're *still* dreaming, Dr. Marcaluso." Elaine told her about their impending date on Tuesday night. "I guess I'm a little nervous," she admitted. She stopped pretending to eat and sipped her lukewarm coffee instead. "I'm not quite sure what to do from here."

"Jump her bones," Maxine said. "It leaves no room for doubt."

Elaine rolled her eyes. "I can't believe I'm asking *you* for advice. She who has sex in the patient loading zone because the elevators are too full first thing in the morning."

Maxine smiled and pushed her empty plate away. "You sound jealous, as well you should." She picked up her coffee cup and studied her friend over the top of it. "What is it about this one?" Maxine asked seriously. "I've seen women trip all over each other trying to get your attention. You've always been a hot commodity out there. Why are you still mooning over someone who doesn't even know you exist?"

"Because in my dreams she's a great kisser."

"Yeah, sure," Maxine said with a smirk. "In your dreams."

Tuesday night Elaine was on time and more nervous than seemed appropriate. Cheryl answered the door dressed in a dark brown skirt with a rust-colored vest and a silk beige blouse. Elaine was momentarily awestruck when she saw her. *Christ, she's gorgeous.*

"My friend the doctor," Cheryl said graciously. "Come in. I'm almost ready."

They decided against doing the tourist thing and agreed on dinner at a nice, quiet restaurant in Monte Vista. Unlike Elaine's dream, Cheryl didn't sit close to her in the car, but all through dinner they kept each other entertained.

"What were you like as a child?" Cheryl asked over a shared piece of cherry cheesecake.

"Curious, smart, stubborn," Elaine said. She laughed suddenly. "A geek. Isn't that what they call kids now? In my day we were nerds, I guess, but girls weren't really called that. You get the picture. I was the one in class who always aced the test and screwed up the curve for everyone else."

Cheryl grinned. "You were the one the rest of us wanted to sit by, hoping to peek at your paper." She touched the end of her fork to her full, perfect bottom lip. "Tell me about your first lover."

And from there they spent the remainder of the evening exchanging coming-out stories and embarrassing adolescent moments. They laughed often, just as in Elaine's dream, and once again they closed the restaurant.

"I can't believe how late it is," Cheryl said during the drive back to her house. "Are you working at the clinic for your mother on Saturday?"

"Oh, yes. She's got my day planned down to the nanosecond."

"Sunday's Gay Fiesta," Cheryl said. "Have you thought about going this year?"

Elaine's heart started thumping. *Is she asking me out? Are the two of us about to make plans over something that's her idea? I'm on call Sunday since Morgan's out of town, but that's no problem. Check on his patients early. Piece of cake.*

"I'm on call Sunday," Elaine said evenly, "but with a beeper, my leash is a bit longer."

"I'm working the political caucus booth for a few hours," Cheryl said, "but other than that I'm free. I'm sure I'll see you there then."

Elaine parked in Cheryl's driveway. She wanted something a bit more definite than *I'm sure I'll see you there.*

"Phoebe's in charge of setting up the booths this year," Cheryl said, "so don't arrive too early or she'll put you to work." She leaned her head back comfortably on the seat and turned in Elaine's direction. "I had a great time tonight."

"You sound surprised."

"I guess I am a little. I've been in such a funk lately." The light from the dash caught Cheryl's smile as she turned her head toward Elaine again. "You're nothing like Mickey."

"Thank you," Elaine said. She was rewarded by a hearty laugh. Their eyes met briefly again, and this was where, if she'd still been dreaming, Elaine would have leaned over to kiss her, but the moment slipped away as Cheryl opened the door and filled the car with unwanted light.

"Till Sunday then," Cheryl said. "Good night."

All the way home Elaine wondered whether or not she was being too passive. *Jump her bones*, Maxine had urged, the Maxine who was never without a lover. Elaine shook her head and sighed. *Maybe Maxine's right.*

Sunday was a beautiful April afternoon. The sun was out and the temperature was expected to be in the low eighties. The music in La Villita Assembly Hall was deafening, but no one seemed to care. Conversations were saved for the festivities on the courtyard where vendors with hot dogs, fajitas, and turkey legs could be found. The only reason the Assembly Hall itself stayed crowded was because that's where the majority of the beer was sold and it was air-conditioned inside.

Elaine saw Phoebe with her BAD ATTITUDE cap on, and she worked her way through the indoor crowd.

"Hey," Phoebe said as she gave her a hug. "How's the skin business today?"

"It's got a few wrinkles." The music was so loud they were practically shouting into each other's ears. "Nice turnout."

"Your mother's working the Coke booth by that enormous speaker over there. The music's so loud that she's wearing earplugs *and* earmuffs. You can't miss her."

Elaine's progress toward the Coke booth was slow and tedious, but she met several women that she knew along the way. Talking loud enough to be heard was impossible, so hugs and hand signals were about all anyone could hope for.

Elaine purchased a Diet Coke from her mother and laughed at the black fuzzy earmuffs that matched Blanche's gray tank top and black Bermuda shorts. Elaine promised to be back later to work a shift with her. Blanche leaned over and shouted in her ear, "I wouldn't wish this detail on anybody. Cheryl's at the caucus booth peddling her wares. Go have some fun. I'll see you later."

Outside in the courtyard was a much more reasonable experience. Another DJ was posted at the far end, sending a blast of music their way, but out in the open the music was doing what it was supposed to do. In one glance Elaine took in the Bobbing for Long Necks booth, the Miss Gay Texas booth that made glitter-monogrammed sashes to one's choosing, the Alamo Couples booth that sold very appropriate fruit drinks, a snow cone and popcorn booth, and a kissing booth. On closer inspection of the kissing booth, Elaine saw Cheryl and Joey, a gay friend of Maxine's, working inside. *Cheryl's selling kisses*, Elaine thought. The line forming in front of the booth was impressive, about ten people, with a nice mixture of both male and female.

Elaine got in line and read the sign on top of the booth: PLAIN KISSES $1 FRENCH KISSES $5. Then in small print below it: TO BENEFIT THE SAN ANTONIO GAY AND LESBIAN POLITICAL CAUCUS.

This was one of Elaine's favorite organizations to donate to. Over the past few years she'd given them thousands of dollars and had sponsored several fund-raisers on her own, along with a few that she and Maxine had done together. Neither of them had a lot of time to help register gay voters or work on political campaigns, so they gave money instead, and their efforts were always appreciated.

Elaine peeked around the people in line in front of her to see how things were going. Small canisters of breath spray and mouthwash were lined up on the tiny ledge in front of the booth. The men in line were kissing Joey, a young Adonis with long, shiny blond hair, and the women were kissing Cheryl. All kisses were platonic pecks on the cheek or an exaggerated pucker on the lips. It was harmless fun for a good cause, and everyone seemed to be having a nice time.

There were three women behind her when Elaine finally made it to the front of the line. Elaine reached in her pocket and pulled out the crisp one-hundred-dollar bill she'd decided the night before to donate. Cheryl and Joey's eyes widened in surprise at the sight of it.

"What do I get for this?" Elaine asked as she held the bill between two fingers.

"Oh, *mercy!*" Joey said. "Even *I'll* kiss you for that!"

"And I'll give you another one if you don't," Elaine informed him.

"Okay, Cheryl, baby," Joey cooed as he elbowed Cheryl in the ribs. "Are you up to this? A hundred bucks."

"I'm speechless," Cheryl murmured. There was a stunned expression on her face, but her eyes were sparkling.

"Let's see," Joey said as he pointed up to the

sign over their heads. "That's either one hundred plain kisses or twenty French ones." He pointed to a box of red plastic tongues with the political caucus logo on each one. Apparently for five dollars a French kiss consisted of a peck on the cheek and a plastic tongue handed over the counter. "Are you *sure* you're up to this, Cheryl?" Joey asked. "You need me to call for reinforcements? We probably wouldn't have any trouble getting volunteers to kiss her."

"No, no," Cheryl said as she began getting her wits together. "I'm fine."

Elaine was nervous and not sure what to do next. She didn't want her first kiss with Cheryl to be under these circumstances, but it was a little late to think about that now. "Who are these for?" Elaine asked Joey as she motioned toward the breath spray, Certs, and mouthwash lined up in front of him. "Me or you?"

"You," Joey said. "We smell good already."

Elaine glanced over at Cheryl, who was laughing and shaking her head.

"My friend the doctor," Cheryl said in a sexy whisper. "What's your pleasure? A hundred regular or twenty premium?"

"Go for the premium," someone in line behind Elaine said.

"Uh . . ."

Before Elaine had a chance to answer, her beeper went off. *This can't be happening!* She tugged on the band of her shorts to check the number on the digital display. *No, no, no. Not now.*

"Is this what life with a doctor would be like?" Cheryl asked.

"Usually not with this doctor." Elaine cleared her

throat nervously. "Sorry. I need to go." A crowd of about fifty people had gathered around the booth already and groaned their disappointment.

"How long can a kiss take?" someone in line said. "You can't leave without *some*thing!"

"Really," Elaine said. "I've gotta go."

Two women stepped out of line and urged Elaine forward with firm grips on her elbows. From there Cheryl reached over the front of the booth and took a handful of Elaine's shirt and pulled her closer.

As Cheryl let go of the shirt, Elaine felt hands move to each side of her head, holding her there, just before Cheryl kissed her deeply with wild, fleeting passion. Cheryl's hands were in Elaine's hair now, and her tongue danced in Elaine's mouth with eager, intense urgency as the crowd began to cheer. Eventually Cheryl pulled away long enough to graze Elaine's ear and throat with her lips. They were both trembling.

"Oh, Jesus," Elaine sighed breathlessly.

"Thanks for the donation," Cheryl whispered in her ear.

"That was worth five hundred, easy," Elaine said. Her legs were so weak she could barely stand up on her own.

"You can write us a check for the other four hundred if you like," Joey suggested.

Cheryl's eyes were locked on her in a smoldering gaze. Elaine was mesmerized and didn't want to leave, but she had to find a telephone and answer the page. She hoped her own eyes were relaying that information as Cheryl let go of her. Elaine turned around and convinced a reluctant crowd to line up in front of the kissing booth and spend some more money. She hurried away and called the hospital from a pay phone near the bathrooms to confirm that she was indeed needed at the hospital. All the way across town her stomach was a tumbling disaster as she replayed the entire incident over and over in her head. *Cheryl kissed me. She really kissed me.*

Elaine got home late and was tired and hungry. She rummaged through her refrigerator and found a can of ginger ale and an apple that had seen better days. She listened to her telephone messages while searching for the remote to the television. Maxine's voice was first, stating she'd meet her for breakfast in the morning at the usual time and place.

"We took your suggestion about sex in the elevator," Maxine said. "I'll give you a full report when I see you."

The next message was from Cheryl. Elaine stopped chewing and listened.

"It's Cheryl. The caucus made six hundred and fifty-three dollars today, largely in part due to your efforts. I've been thinking about you all afternoon. I was wondering if we could have dinner again. Give me a call when you get a chance."

Elaine stretched out on the sofa and closed her eyes. This was too good to be true. She picked up the phone and dialed Cheryl's number. *You deserve a break, Marcaluso. Make the most of this while you can.*

Cheryl answered on the first ring. "Hello."

"Hi. It's me. Your friend the doctor." Elaine relaxed a little when she heard Cheryl's easy laughter.

"Joey and I made more on our shift than any of the other caucus members. We've both got exhausted lips." She lowered her voice. "I'm sorry you had to leave when you did."

"Yeah, well," Elaine said, "I've always had buzzard luck and incredible timing."

"How about dinner tomorrow? I think we should talk about a few things."

"What sort of things?" Elaine asked.

"You. Me. All sorts of things. Most of all, that kiss. I can't stop thinking about it. So . . . how does tomorrow at seven sound? Will you pick me up?"

"Yes," Elaine said. "Sure. Tomorrow at seven. I'll see you then."

Chapter Seven

"Sit down," Elaine said as she sipped her coffee the next morning. Maxine's grin hinted at a sex-before-sunup day already. "And I don't wanna hear anything about love in the elevator, okay? I'm sure it was great, so there's no need to elaborate."

"Sex in an elevator has its ups and downs, my friend," Maxine said.

Elaine opened her menu and groaned. "I'm having dinner with Cheryl tonight. She called *me* this time."

"Hmm. Is that so? I take it you haven't jumped her bones yet."

"No. Not yet."

"Tonight maybe?"

"We're weeks away from that."

"*Weeks?*" Maxine repeated, horrified. Her beeper went off, and she checked the number on the display and dug in her purse for her cellular phone all in one fluid motion. "The Gillespie baby, I betcha," she said as she extended the little antenna on the phone and punched in the numbers. While waiting for someone to answer, Maxine scanned her menu. "Dr. Weston returning a page," she said.

Elaine watched her with a raised eyebrow, wondering how often Betina, Maxine's lover, found herself alone in a restaurant with two meals to eat and pay for. *That's probably why they spend so much time making love in the car. Maxine's never in one place long enough for anything else.*

"How far apart?"

Elaine closed her menu and sipped her coffee.

"Tell her I'm on my way. It'll make her feel better." Maxine closed her menu also and motioned for the waitress. "We're ready to order," she said as she pushed the little antenna down on the portable phone and checked her beeper again.

They placed their orders and fiddled with their coffee.

"So," Maxine said after a moment. "When was the last time you had sex, Dr. Marcaluso?" Then she added, "Uh, with another person."

"Very funny," Elaine grumbled. "And that's none of your business, by the way."

"That long, huh?" Maxine smiled outrageously. "What are you saving it for? You're making me nuts with all this waiting."

74

Elaine sighed and toyed with her silverware. "I kissed her yesterday. It cost me a hundred bucks, but I kissed her."

"Cheryl? You kissed *Cheryl*?" Maxine folded her hands in front of her on the table. "Back up and start over, already."

Elaine told her about the kissing booth and the hundred-dollar donation and getting paged just before she was supposed to get her hundred kisses.

"Wait a minute," Maxine said. "You got *paged*? On a *Sunday*? What the hell did you get paged for? Did the mayor find a pimple on his ass or something? Dermatologists *never* get paged!"

"I was covering for Morgan. He's got a patient in the hospital who's allergic to everything we're giving him. He was fine when I checked on him Sunday morning, but then he got worse later."

"I see. Hmm. So how was the kiss?"

Elaine closed her eyes as her stomach did its usual tumbling act whenever she thought about Cheryl at any length. "It was wonderful," she whispered, her voice full of emotion. "We're having dinner tonight to talk about it." At Maxine's skeptical look, Elaine added, "If I rush into anything, I'm afraid I'll screw it up." She sat back in the booth and tossed a lock of hair out of her eyes. "I guess all that discussion about Mickey has got me on edge."

"What's Cheryl saying about Mickey?"

"It's not what *Cheryl* is saying that worries me," Elaine snapped as she looked up at her. "Not yet, anyway. It's *you*. 'A fucking genius in the sack' and 'They'll be back together in a month.' Mickey this and Mickey that. Christ, Maxine. What if you're right?"

"So now it's *my* fault your confidence is in the toilet?"

Elaine rolled her eyes and shook her head. "My confidence is fine," she said, making an effort to keep her voice down. "I've got a plan, and I don't need your advice, okay? Just let me do this my way."

"What's the plan?"

"A few weeks of wining and dining. Flowers and candy. A little romance. The whole bit."

"Then you'll jump her bones?"

Elaine shrugged. "Then I'll at least be ready to think about it."

It had been a busy day, and under normal circumstances Elaine would've been tired and grouchy, but these were far from normal circumstances. She had a date with Cheryl Trinidad, a date that Cheryl herself had called and suggested. Nothing else seemed to matter.

Cheryl answered the door with something similar to that smoldering look Elaine had left her with at the kissing booth the day before. There was magic in the air as they slowly checked each other out.

"Come in," Cheryl said. "I'm late feeding Cardigan. I'll just be a minute."

Elaine waited in the living room and studied the books in a bookcase near the fireplace. She realized after a moment that she was looking at a fine collection of first editions. There was, however, one slim volume in the middle of the shelf that caught her attention. She selected the copy of *101 Uses for a Dead Cat* and opened it up to read:

Merry Christmas, Cardigan. Here's a glimpse at your future. Ha-ha. Just kidding!
                                    Love, Mickey

Elaine smiled at her sister's sick sense of humor. Mickey had never been much of an animal lover. Cardigan was probably doing cartwheels over this breakup. Elaine returned the book to the shelf when she heard Cheryl in the hallway.

"Do we have reservations somewhere?"

Elaine stuck her hands in her pockets. "I didn't think to make any. Did you?"

There was a playfulness in Cheryl's eyes as she slowly moved across the room. Elaine was struck once again by how graceful and beautiful she was. *Why would anyone consciously hurt this woman?* she wondered.

"You're very punctual," Cheryl said. "Have I mentioned how much I like that?"

Elaine shook her head. She wasn't sure exactly where her voice had gone, but she knew better than to try to use it right then. Cheryl was standing in front of her now, so close that Elaine caught a hint of her perfume.

"Are we in a hurry?" Cheryl asked.

"No," Elaine said. "Not at all." Their eyes met again, and Elaine could feel her heart thumping.

"My friend the doctor," Cheryl said, tilting her head to get a better look at her. She reached over and gently ran the tip of her finger from the edge of Elaine's mouth to her cheek. Cheryl's fingers brushed the front of her hair. Elaine's searching, penetrating eyes held her captive. "We'd better get going before I do something totally out of character."

"Like what?" Elaine whispered. Her stomach began to tumble again, and all senses in her body snapped to attention.

"Like throw you on the sofa and have my way with you."

Elaine leaned closer and touched Cheryl's lips with her own. Before Elaine knew what was happening, Cheryl pulled her into her arms for a deep kiss that left them both breathless. At the mercy of Cheryl's mouth on her throat, Elaine struggled for composure. Seconds later, Cheryl's tongue became urgent and demanding. Her hands moved swiftly over Elaine's body.

"The sofa's for kids," Cheryl whispered. "Come to bed with me." She took Elaine's hand and led the way to her bedroom where kissing became the center of the universe. Long kisses that Elaine had waited a lifetime for, kisses that made her weak with desire.

Clothes were hastily removed when neither of them could get close enough. Elaine wanted to touch her everywhere and at the same time loved the way Cheryl's hands caressed her body. *This is heaven, Marcaluso. You finally made it to heaven.*

Cheryl's body was flawless in the light filtering in from a nearby bathroom. Her full breasts, flat stomach, and long, shapely legs were all as perfect as Elaine imagined them to be. Cheryl pulled away from her long enough to toss the cover back from the bed. She brought Elaine down with her as their soft, cool bodies melted together. Elaine felt light-headed and so incredibly lucky that she thought she might cry. This was so much better than any dream she could ever have. Cheryl was on top of her, moving against her, wanting this as much as Elaine did. *Pure heaven.*

Cheryl's aggression was a surprise, like discovering one's Sunday school teacher had an active sex life. Elaine was close to a sensory overload as Cheryl's hands moved over her body. Passion and lust were no longer distinguishable. Elaine had waited years for this moment, had played this very scene over in her mind a hundred times. She didn't want to come yet — it was too soon. She wanted to prolong this moment forever, but she knew that she was close to the edge already. She rolled Cheryl over on her back and delighted in Cheryl's hands, which were once again caressing her, before she reached around to firmly rub her back.

Their kisses were wild now, and full of deep exchanges of tongue and unconscious murmurs. Elaine searched for Cheryl's breasts and then eagerly licked and sucked those hard nipples. She reached down and urged Cheryl's legs open, letting her fingers dart through damp curls and delicate folds to her wet, pulsating center.

"I think I came when you kissed me in the living room," Cheryl said in a husky whisper.

"You think?" Elaine replied with a smile. "The next time you come, Ms. Trinidad, you'll know it."

Elaine's fingers danced over glistening flesh as she moved down Cheryl's stomach, kissing her everywhere along the way. She wanted to drive this woman crazy with her mouth and feel her shudder with pleasure over and over again before they were finished. Elaine settled between Cheryl's legs. She reached up, found her hands, and placed them on her head. Her invitation encouraged Cheryl to open her legs farther and grip Elaine's hair firmly.

It was marvelous having Cheryl move against her this way and being able to hear those deep, throaty moans. Elaine was surprised at how aroused she herself had become so quickly. Undulating hips responded to Elaine's insistent probing, and Cheryl's body became reckless as she tossed and thrashed about. Her hands held Elaine right where Cheryl needed her. Elaine could feel her own body responding to some feral, desperate need as she savored the taste of her.

Seconds later Cheryl came with a low, husky moan that brought a smile to Elaine's face. The fingers released her hair and fluttered around her head like sugarplum fairies.

"Come here," Cheryl whispered breathlessly. "Oh, god, Elaine. Come here so I can hold you."

Elaine kissed the inside of Cheryl's thigh and dried her mouth on the bedspread beside her. She was in Cheryl's arms quickly as frantic kisses covered her face and forehead.

Cheryl's eyes were closed and her breathing ragged. She had the drowsy, exhausted, after-sex look that Elaine cherished on a woman. When she could breathe normally again, she opened her eyes and kissed Elaine tenderly on the lips. "I knew it would be this way with you." Cheryl kissed her again and then reached over to turn the lamp on beside the bed. "I want to see you when I make love to you."

"There's no hurry. It's okay. We've got all night."

Jesus. I'm so ready that the minute you touch *me it'll be all over!*

Cheryl turned on her side and propped her head up with her hand as she looked down at Elaine's nude body. She cupped one of Elaine's breasts and ran her tongue across the nipple. "You're right. There's no hurry," Cheryl said with a smile. "Should I taste you first, or touch you first? Or does it matter since I plan to do both several times before we're through."

Elaine closed her eyes and shook her head. "Tasting's my favorite," she said shyly. "And it should take you about fifteen seconds at the most the way I'm feeling right now."

"Then that's where I'll start," Cheryl whispered. "Get ready for a long night."

"But you don't understand," Cheryl said with a throaty chuckle. "Twice has always been my limit without a vibrator."

"Obviously no longer the case," Elaine said as she nuzzled her neck. They'd been at it for hours already, and neither seemed ready to stop yet. "Besides, didn't I carry all your sex toys out of here and take them to my mother's?"

Cheryl was kissing her again and working a knee between Elaine's legs.

"That's a negative," Cheryl said. "I gave away a can opener. I kept the toys. All dishwasher safe, too. A great collection for any occasion." She hugged her and pushed thick, unruly hair away from Elaine's eyes and forehead. "Something wonderful is happening to me, Elaine. This is totally out of character for me." Cheryl hugged her again and kissed the top of her head. "I think I would've done something really crazy if I hadn't been able to touch you when you got here earlier."

She laughed and rubbed her cheek against Elaine's soft hair. Elaine kissed her throat and shoulder, hoping to say with her body what she felt in her heart. Cheryl rolled Elaine on top of her and slipped a knee between her legs.

"Where do you keep those toys, Ms. Trinidad?" Elaine whispered. "We've got three hours before that alarm's going off."

"I couldn't possibly have another one," she said as Elaine's lips gently covered her nipple. "Mmm. But then maybe I'm no longer totally aware of the situation." Cheryl wove her fingers through Elaine's thick black hair and said, "The drawer on the nightstand. Ms. Silkie the Wonder Wand is my favorite."

Chapter Eight

Elaine was surprised to see Maxine already at the restaurant when she arrived. Much to her dismay, a glance at her watch confirmed that *she* was late rather than Maxine being early. Elaine fluffed up the back of her still damp hair. Taking a shower with Cheryl this morning would've been an excellent idea had they not spent so much time necking under the spray. Elaine could almost feel her body glow whenever she thought about Cheryl. If she had to, she'd be able to function for months on memory alone after last night.

"I thought I had the wrong restaurant," Maxine said. "I've never beat you here before."

"I got held up," Elaine said.

"Are you okay? You look different this morning."

"I'm fine," Elaine said. "I've been —"

"Wait until you hear what happened to me last night," Maxine said. She had a gleam in her eye that alerted Elaine to an upcoming tale of sexual adventure, but the waitress pouring coffee and taking their orders momentarily interrupted them. "Betina has a friend who works at Sea World," Maxine said once the waitress had gone. "Have you listened to the news this morning? Did you see the headlines in the paper?"

Elaine shook her head. Cheryl had been the only thing on her mind.

"We were there when Baby Shamu was born last night!" Maxine exclaimed. "It was incredible!"

"Baby Shamu? The whale? You're kidding, right? That's what has you this excited?"

"It was a media event," Maxine said, a bit miffed at Elaine's lack of enthusiasm. "We had special badges and everything."

"Special badges. Wow." Elaine laughed. *Jesus, I feel good this morning.* "I'm relieved to know that you two can go out in public and keep your clothes on when you have to. That's great."

Maxine raised an eyebrow and smirked. "I haven't finished my story yet, Dr. Marcaluso. While everyone else was at the baby shower afterward, my little Betina and I christened Shamu Stadium. The acoustics there are fabulous, by the way. It was a titillating experience, as they say."

"Shamu Stadium? You and Betina in —"

"Shamu Stadium," Maxine finished for her. "She had me right there in the wet zone, honey. Front row center. It was out of this world."

"It's called the *splash* zone, not the *wet* zone," Elaine reminded her.

"Trust me on this one, Dr. Marcaluso. It was the *wet* zone by the time *we* finished with it." Maxine slowly ran the tip of her tongue over her glossy top lip and shook her head. "I go to work every day just so I can get some rest, I tell you." She picked up her coffee cup. "So. How are things with you? Has there been any progress on the Cheryl Trinidad front, so to speak?"

Elaine leaned back against the booth and smiled at her. "We made love last night," she said quietly.

"You *what*?" Maxine yelped. She set her cup down, spilling a large majority of its contents all over the saucer. "Did you really?"

Elaine nodded.

"Why'd you let me go on and on about that stupid *fish*? Tell me everything, and don't leave out a word."

They drank their coffee and talked while Elaine answered a barrage of questions sprinkled with occasional loud hoots of delight from Maxine. Elaine refused to discuss the intimate details of their night of passion, even though Maxine tried to pry them out of her several times.

"Well," Maxine said with a little smirk. "I've always admired your patience." They clinked their cups in a toast. "Good things happen to those who wait, Dr. Marcaluso. And you're way overdue for this one."

"That's not what I remember you saying years

ago," Elaine reminded her. "Your philosophy then was that *nothing* happens to those who wait."

Maxine's warm smile was contagious. "And occasionally I've been known to be wrong."

Late that same afternoon, Elaine rang Cheryl's doorbell. Her heart felt like an out-of-control jump rope slapping in her chest. She couldn't remember two-thirds of what she had done all day other than think about the night before and fantasize about what she planned to do to Cheryl later. Elaine waved at the face peeking though the drapes, and she could tell by the rattle of the lock that Cheryl was just as anxious to see her. The door opened wide, and Cheryl reached for Elaine's hand to pull her inside.

"I've been looking forward to this all day," she said into the soft hollow of Elaine's neck. The door closed behind them, and Cheryl was in her arms kissing her feverishly.

Elaine's body responded on cue as Cheryl's hand slipped inside her shirt and rubbed her breast. Elaine could hear herself uttering tiny wordless sounds that went along with the string of somersaults coursing through her stomach. Cheryl's passion matched her own, and the need to feel skin seemed to come over them both at the same time. They were locked in a deep kiss, with zippers and buttons cooperating as they helped each other out of their clothes.

"Oh, god, you feel good," Cheryl whispered. "Come to bed with me." She didn't let go of Elaine's hand as they headed for the bedroom, but once they were there, Cheryl undressed her near the foot of the bed. "Let's take it slow this time," she whispered as she kissed Elaine's throat and bare shoulder. They were both trembling with emotion. She touched Elaine's earlobe with the tip of her tongue and slowly sucked it into her mouth.

Elaine closed her eyes and pressed her body against Cheryl's, needing to feel as much of her as possible. *To hell with this slow business,* Elaine thought, and helped get the last of their clothing off.

Cheryl turned the light on beside the bed and then kissed her fully on the mouth. After a moment she took Elaine's face in her hands and whispered, "The things I want to do to you."

Elaine couldn't speak. She felt as if she were on fire from the lust in Cheryl's voice and the look in her eyes. Elaine urged her back on the bed. Words were scrambled in her head as she rolled on top of her and buried her face between Cheryl's breasts. This was the only person in the world who could make her speechless, but Elaine wasn't beyond uttering short phrases.

"I could kiss you for hours," Elaine said. She took a nipple into her mouth and felt a new surge of desire when Cheryl's body arched to meet her. As she worked her way along Cheryl's stomach, kissing her cool flesh and circling her navel with a darting tongue, Cheryl's hands in Elaine's hair coaxed her downward. Cheryl opened her legs, making an exquisite sound when Elaine's mouth touched her.

Elaine was in absolute heaven, and Cheryl was close behind. Probing, licking, sucking, Elaine slipped two fingers inside of her and let her tongue seek and search on its own accord. Cheryl's fingers had Elaine's hair in a firm grip, and her hips began moving in a desperate crescendo of pleasure. She came quickly, but hard, and her body shook with the effort.

Cheryl stopped moving a long time before her fingers relaxed around Elaine's head. Elaine liked being there, between Cheryl's legs with her face wet and her tongue wiser from the experience. She kissed Cheryl's sweet, wet center and the inside of her damp thighs. She could feel Cheryl trying to tug on her ear in an attempt to pull her up.

"Come here," Cheryl said. "Come here where I can hold you."

Elaine took her time and kissed her way back up Cheryl's body. She cherished that heavy-lidded drunken look and hoped to see it several times again before the night was over.

"You're very good at that," Cheryl said in a small, sleepy voice. She tried to laugh and then hugged her with what little strength she had left. "*Very* good." Her fingertips brushed stray locks away from Elaine's eyes. "My lover the doctor," she whispered, and then tightened her arms around her.

My lover the doctor, Elaine thought as a lump formed in her throat. *You're not just someone she's sleeping with, Marcaluso. She called you her lover.*

She kissed Elaine on the forehead as her hand moved down to Elaine's breast. Cheryl kissed her again with such surprising, avid desire that it took Elaine's breath away.

Cheryl's lips moved to Elaine's throat after a moment. "Turn over on your side," she said.

Elaine could hear her own ragged breathing as she followed instructions. She felt Cheryl's breasts pressing against her back, nipples hard and ready.

Cheryl reached around and caressed Elaine's nipples while she rubbed her own against her shoulder. She moved Elaine's hair away from the side of her face and ran her tongue along an ear. Cheryl's warm breath and light kisses were adding more fuel to the fire smoldering between Elaine's legs. Cheryl's hand rubbed Elaine's breasts again and then moved down the smooth, flat stomach, eventually lingering at the edge of her pubic hair.

"Open your legs for me," Cheryl whispered. Her lips never stopped kissing Elaine's face, throat, shoulder. Her lips were moving and searching for new avenues of pleasure.

Elaine loved the way Cheryl talked to her when she was aroused. *Come to bed with me. Open your legs for me.* Never a question — always a direct and provocative request.

"I've never been sexually aggressive before," Cheryl whispered. Her fingers slipped through damp curls and spread Elaine open, exposing her sex. "But with you I'm in such a hurry all the time. I can't touch you fast enough or long enough." That exquisite tongue kept nipping and darting around Elaine's ear, making her shiver with anticipation and pleasure. "Turn over on your back. I want to see you."

Elaine gladly did as she was told and felt that familiar roller coaster in her stomach as Cheryl leaned over and circled a nipple with that eager tongue.

"The day at the kissing booth," Cheryl said, "I was so nervous when I saw you get in line. I knew what kind of kiss I wanted to give you." With her free hand she inched along Elaine's stomach, keeping the fingers of her other hand inside. She moved down between Elaine's legs and flicked her tongue along the inside of her thigh, all the while running her thumb up and down her wet center.

"You're beautiful, Elaine," she whispered. "I knew it would be this way with you."

Elaine was mesmerized by her voice, and then startled by the intensity of feeling that oozed through her body. Cheryl's mouth was warm and hungry, and that tongue so greedy as it searched and seized. Elaine was consumed by sensation and oblivious to everything else but Cheryl between her legs feasting on her, licking and sucking. Elaine thrashed around the bed, her hands sifting through Cheryl's hair. When the fireworks exploded behind her eyelids and she recognized the panting and yelling as her own, Elaine collapsed on a pillow and tried to catch her breath. Orgasms weren't new to her, but this experience deserved a place of its own in her memoirs.

Cheryl was beside her now, kissing her cheek and brushing stray locks of hair away from her eyes. "Turn over," she whispered.

Elaine attempted to smile, but the effort was exhausting. "I don't think I can move," she managed to say. "I'm surprised I can still breathe on my own."

Cheryl chuckled and gave her a nudge. "Turn over. I'll make it worth your while."

Elaine turned over on her stomach in a drowsy, sex-induced stupor, but she moaned her approval when Cheryl straddled her body and rested comfortably across her lower back.

She began rubbing a strawberry-scented lotion into Elaine's shoulders and neck, warming it in the palm of her hand first. "You taste good," Cheryl said. "Has anyone ever told you that?"

"No," Elaine said. Her eyes were closed and the need for a respirator had passed — she was breathing normally again. "Jesus, this feels wonderful."

Cheryl leaned over and brushed her nipples against Elaine. "We haven't even started yet," she whispered. More lotion was applied, and slow, deep rubbing up and down Elaine's back and shoulders relaxed her completely. Cheryl's fingertips and hands were like magic on her body; Elaine could stay there forever. The next thing she knew, Elaine heard the hum of a vibrator, and Ms. Silkie the Wonder Wand was massaging a shoulder and easing what little tension there was around her neck.

"Mmm," Elaine purred. The sound alone was exciting, but she was still in no condition to do anything about it.

Cheryl would lean over occasionally and whisper something like "Nice shoulders" or "Kissing you can make me come."

She moved the vibrator over Elaine's ribs and teased the sides of her breasts. Cheryl's voice was sexy when she whispered, and those nipples grazing Elaine's skin continued to send shivers through her body.

Elaine wanted to see her, and she turned over on her back with both of them shifting positions. Cheryl settled on top of her again and straddled Elaine's waist, still resting on her knees. She ran the tip of the humming vibrator under Elaine's firm, perky breasts and smiled down at her with humor and desire etched in her eyes. She moved the vibrator along the side of Elaine's right breast and shook her hair off her bare shoulders.

"Touch yourself with it," Elaine said. "I'd like to watch you."

"That wasn't the original plan," Cheryl whispered.

Elaine reached up and cupped Cheryl's breasts and whispered in return, "Making love has no agenda."

"Then you touch me with it," Cheryl said. She eased the Wonder Wand into Elaine's hand and let her cool fingers trail along Elaine's sensitive flesh.

Elaine moved the vibrator across Cheryl's stomach and then down to the inside of her thigh. A decisive moan escaped from Cheryl's throat as Elaine slipped the vibrator between her legs. Elaine's attention remained riveted on Cheryl's expression — her eyes closed, lips parted, head thrown back. *Ecstasy in motion*, Elaine thought as she watched her, touched her, listened to her. *Is this what we all look like just before it happens? We're so busy doing other things to one another that we never get to witness this moment.*

Cheryl's hand covered Elaine's and took control of the vibrator. "Touch my breasts," she said, and then with her other hand she guided Elaine to squeeze her nipples. The variations of *oh* started deep in Cheryl's throat and escalated to a delicious, earthy moan. Her body rocked steadily in preamble to orgasm, and Elaine witnessed everything from its inception to its glorious finale.

Afterward Elaine turned the vibrator off, and she

stuck it under a pillow out of the way. Cheryl was beside her now, lethargic and exhausted.

"Thank you for sharing that with me," Elaine whispered. Her voice was full of emotion as she rubbed a tear-stained cheek against Cheryl's forehead. "Thank you."

Chapter Nine

Elaine followed the smell of fresh coffee all the way to the kitchen where she found Cheryl in a long robe and matching, fuzzy house shoes. Elaine had been able to locate all of her clothes from the night before, even though having to put them back on again wasn't very appealing. She took the coffee cup Cheryl handed to her and set it beside Cheryl's cup already on the counter. They began kissing almost immediately, sweet good-morning kisses that made Elaine all warm and squirmy inside.

"Do you have time for breakfast?" Cheryl asked.

"Not really." Elaine pulled the sash on Cheryl's robe and slipped her arms around her nude body. "I can't believe I forgot to bring a change of clothes." Now she had to rush home, take a shower, and jump right back into morning traffic.

"But you'll bring them tonight, won't you?"

"Oh, yes. Definitely." Elaine kissed her throat and the soft hollow of Cheryl's neck and shoulder. "I have to be in Saint Louis this weekend for a conference. I'm leaving tomorrow afternoon. Can you come with me?"

"I've got a meeting with the city manager on Saturday," Cheryl said, the disappointment evident in her voice. "We're discussing library funding. I can't get out of it."

Elaine was presenting a paper at the conference, which made it something she couldn't get out of either.

Cheryl put her arms around Elaine's neck and let their foreheads touch. "When will you be back?"

"Sunday afternoon around five."

She kissed the tip of Elaine's nose and nudged it playfully with her own. "You'd better get all the sleep you'll need on the flight back, darling, because you won't be getting any Sunday night. I can promise you that."

Darling. She called you darling, *Marcaluso!*

"We'll have a nice quiet dinner here tonight," Cheryl said. "I haven't been much of a hostess since I've gotten you in bed."

"Food I can get anywhere," Elaine whispered, and kissed her again.

* * * * *

After a busy morning treating a case of acne, a severe case of heat rash in a groin area, and some extensive wart removals, Elaine enjoyed her second cup of coffee of the day. There usually wasn't much time between patients, but someone had called and canceled just before lunch, giving her an opportunity to read over her paper again. Public speaking wasn't one of Elaine's strong points; it was something she had to work at. But she felt certain that a few run-throughs on the way to Saint Louis would keep her from embarrassing herself when the time came.

She checked her watch and realized she had twenty minutes to get something for lunch if she was going to eat today. She opened her office door and found Mickey standing there.

"Holy shit," Mickey yelled. "You scared me."

"What are you doing here?" Elaine was confused for a moment. One of those what's-wrong-with-this-picture cartoons kept popping in her head. She hadn't seen Mickey in three months, and as far as Elaine could remember, Mickey had never been to her office before — even for its grand opening two years ago.

Elaine opened her door wider and motioned toward the chair in front of her desk. *You can kiss lunch good-bye, Marcaluso.*

"I've gotta be in court in forty-five minutes," Mickey said as she sat down and got comfortable. Her gray power suit was tailored to perfection, the cut of the jacket and the length of the skirt. Mickey knew how to dress for success. Her clothes were expensive. She actually *looked* like a lawyer.

As Elaine watched her sister, she tried to imagine what women found attractive about her. Mickey's hair was the same color as Elaine's, jet black and thick, only Mickey wore hers fashionably short. She reeked of confidence and had a sense of humor that could border on the bizarre, but Mickey had something else that Elaine had never quite been able to identify. Other than both of them being lesbians, having the same two parents, and at one time being in love with the same woman, they had absolutely nothing in common.

"Why has your car been in Cheryl's driveway two nights in a row?" Mickey asked, getting right to the point.

Elaine was momentarily stunned by the question, and she knew that her mouth had to be gaping open. They stared at one another, both waiting for Elaine to say something.

"Answer the question," Mickey said slowly in her cool, courtroom voice.

"Where my car stays is none of your business." Elaine's mind raced as she thought about what this could possibly mean — Mickey's showing up here at the office this way, Mickey's watching Cheryl's house, Mickey's giving a rat's ass what Cheryl did now or whom she did it with. Mickey was jealous; Elaine could see it in her eyes. And this was *not* good news.

"Why are you driving by Cheryl's house at night?" Elaine queried in return.

Mickey was startled by the question and shifted uneasily in her chair. "Well, it's on my way —"

"It's on your way *no*where, so don't give me that."

"It sure as hell hasn't taken you very long to —"

"Answer my question, Mickey. Why are you driving by Cheryl's house at night?"

Mickey stood up suddenly and pulled her keys

from her jacket pocket. Her jaw was set and her cheeks were flushed. She looked away from Elaine and said, "It was a mistake coming here." She was across the room and had the door open before Elaine could move away from her desk. Once she was alone, Elaine felt a sense of relief, but as she sat there staring at the door, two things kept flashing in her head: *Mickey's jealous. And why is she driving by Cheryl's house at night?*

Elaine went home after work to pack for the conference and to make sure her cat had enough of everything to keep him out of trouble for a few days. Her neighbor promised to check on him Saturday, but Elaine would have to come back home at some point on Sunday to make sure all was well. She'd also need to get a change of clothes for work Monday morning. Elaine wondered if Cheryl would be willing to stay the night over here on Sunday. *You'd better put clean sheets on the bed just in case. You still need to make a good impression.*

Elaine arrived at Cheryl's house a little after seven to the savory smell of onions and garlic drifting through the house. Her stomach growled so loud that it was embarrassing.

"I'm starving," Elaine said. "I missed lunch today."

Cheryl's lips nibbled at her earlobe, sending a shiver through Elaine's body. "What time do you have to leave tomorrow?" Cheryl asked.

"Three." Her stomach grumbled again and made them both laugh. She let Cheryl lead her down the hallway to the kitchen.

"I'd better feed you before it's too late," Cheryl said.

They ate by candlelight and had wine with their meal. Cheryl had prepared chicken fricassee with wild rice and steamed broccoli. The table was impressive with pale yellow place mats and matching napkins.

"Save room for dessert," Cheryl said a while later.

She brought out a small, picture-perfect apple cobbler, smelling of cinnamon and still warm. Elaine was known for her healthy appetite. She truly enjoyed food and was grateful that she'd been blessed with a metabolism that compensated for her bad eating habits.

"What a wonderful meal," Elaine said once the emergency was over.

Cheryl smiled. "It helps that you were famished, I'm sure." Her eyes took in Elaine with a subtle, lingering look. "I hope it was worth the wait," she said huskily.

Elaine felt the whoosh of the roller coaster in her stomach again. *Yes,* she wanted to say. *You've been well worth the wait.* She could feel her heart begin to race and the heat rush through her as Cheryl reached for her hand.

"The things I plan to do to you later," Cheryl whispered.

They both got up from the table at the same time. Elaine leaned over and blew out the candles. "Tell me about these plans you have," she said.

"They're sexual in nature." Cheryl's lips were on Elaine's throat, sending delightful surges of pleasure between her legs.

"All the better," Elaine whispered.

"Are you sure you don't want me to take you to the airport this afternoon?" Cheryl asked the next morning.

Elaine tilted her head back, encouraging Cheryl to continue kissing her neck. "We couldn't do this at the airport," Elaine said, "and besides, I like remembering you all cuddly and sleepy." She kissed her lightly on the lips. "I'll call you from the hotel tonight to make sure you're missing me."

Their eyes met, and Elaine could see the effect her words had. Cheryl's look asked the unspoken question, *How could you think I wouldn't miss you?* It was a powerful, reassuring look.

Neither had spoken about it yet, but Elaine knew that Cheryl was falling in love with her. Things just felt too right between them. And besides, Elaine wasn't sure what she would do if Cheryl *didn't* fall in love with her. She forced that particular thought out of her head and refused to dwell on it.

As Cheryl's fingers moved through the front of Elaine's hair, she could see the beginning of a smile on her face. "Off with you before you have to get dressed all over again," Cheryl whispered. She hugged her and then straightened the collar on Elaine's blouse. "Until Sunday, my sweet."

* * * * *

Elaine went over her paper twice on the flight to Saint Louis. She knew most of the material by heart now and reminded herself again what an honor it was to be selected this way. Maxine's observation at lunch that afternoon, however, hadn't sounded quite so inspiring.

"It's the year of the woman, Dr. Marcaluso," she'd said between bites of her chef salad. "These conferences have been taking hits for not recognizing enough women. We'll all be presenting papers now. You watch."

The hotel lobby had a huge sign directing them where to report for the conference, and they checked into the hotel. The place was crawling with dermatologists, and Elaine recognized several faces from other such events. The mixer was interesting, and a few even asked about Elaine's paper. Her name had appeared in the conference brochure that had gone out the previous month.

Once in her room for the evening, she unpacked her clothes and hung them in the closet. She was tired and kicked her shoes off before glancing at her watch. It was seven-thirty already. Cheryl was probably home by now. Just dialing the number gave her a silly thrill.

"Hi," she said when Cheryl answered the phone. "It's me."

"And how's the Gateway to the West treating you today?"

"Fine," Elaine said as she piled pillows up behind her. "I'm checked into the hotel and signed into the conference, and I've been adequately wined and cheesed. Now for the really important question," she said seriously. "And this is the main reason why I called." She lowered her voice and asked in her sexiest whisper, "What are you wearing?"

"What am I *wearing*?" Cheryl repeated with a laugh. "Oh, my. Is this one of those calls?"

"It could be." Elaine was amazed at how much better she felt just hearing Cheryl's voice. *You've got it bad, Marcaluso. Real bad.* "First tell me where you are," Elaine said. "The living room? The kitchen?"

"The bedroom," Cheryl said. "I'm sprucing the place up a bit."

"The bedroom. Mmm. My favorite." Elaine smiled when she heard Cheryl's laughter.

"Cardigan found a box of Kleenex and emptied it for me," Cheryl said. "My bedroom's a white, fluffy mess right now." She still had a touch of amusement in her voice as she added, "And I'm wearing gray sweatpants, white socks, and my purple T-shirt from the Houston Lesbian Conference . . . my let's-clean-house outfit. It's really a lot more chic than it sounds." She paused for a moment and said, "I clean house when I'm lonely, by the way."

Elaine's stomach did a little flip. "Are you lonely now?"

"It's silly, I know." Cheryl was quiet for a moment and then she asked, "Is it too soon for this, Elaine?"

"Too soon for what?"

Cheryl sighed and laughed again. "Too soon for me to be *cleaning* already when you've only been gone a few hours. Please, let's talk about something else. Tell me about the conference. Anything interesting going on? Or just the usual speakers, work-shops, banquet, etcetera, etcetera."

"That pretty much says it all."

"Someone's at the door," Cheryl said. "Joey's supposed to bring some flyers by for the caucus meeting."

"Then I'd better let you go. Boy Wonder waits for no woman. I'll see you Sunday." She hung up and lay on the bed with the phone beside her. It promised to be a long weekend.

In her room later that night, Elaine had tuned to *Jurassic Park* on the TV but had lost interest in it right away. She got ready for bed and then dozed while reading an article on benign skin tumors. She decided to call it a night at around eleven and officially went to bed. Hours later, from the deep, dark recesses of sleep, Elaine heard the telephone ringing.

She didn't even bother opening her eyes as she felt around on the small table beside the bed. It had to be a wrong number.

"Hello," she mumbled.

"Hi," Cheryl said. "It's me."

Even in her sleep Elaine recognized the voice. She smiled and felt all warm inside again.

"Is this my lover the librarian?" Elaine asked.

"Yes, it is. You were asleep," Cheryl said, her voice soft and low. "And you'd better be alone."

Elaine chuckled and sank deeper into her pillows.

"So," Cheryl said. "What are you wearing?"

I love this woman, Elaine thought as she chuckled again and stretched her warm, sleepy body under the covers.

"Compared to last night, I'm severely over-dressed."

"I miss you," Cheryl whispered. "I just wanted you to know that. Good night. Go back to sleep."

Elaine heard the phone click and the connection break. Something wonderful had just happened. Sweet dreams came easily after that.

Chapter Ten

Elaine tried to stay interested in the workshop, but her mind kept drifting back to Cheryl. They'd talked briefly that morning, sleepy dialogue laced with teasing, sexual innuendo. Elaine remembered almost telling Cheryl at one point that she was in love with her, but now she was glad she hadn't. There was something nagging at her about how Mickey fit into all of this. A month wasn't a very long time when it came to breaking up.

Elaine scanned the schedule in her virtually untouched conference packet and familiarized herself with what would be happening the rest of the weekend. Her presentation had gone well earlier, and with that out of the way, she hoped the remaining part of the conference would be somewhat stress-free. *Maybe you'll even learn something while you're here, Marcaluso.*

She glanced at her watch and quietly collected her things; she'd promised to meet someone for lunch. She slipped out of the workshop and into the busy hallway.

Don Garrett and Elaine had been dermatology residents in New York five years ago. During their training those first few months, Don had spent a good portion of what little spare time he had trying to convince Elaine that he was the man who could change her life. His classic good looks, along with his family's old money, had always gotten him anything he wanted, and Dr. Elaine Marcaluso had quickly become number one on his new wish list back then.

"You can't be," Elaine remembered him saying when she first told him she was a lesbian. The shock on his face had been genuine. Elaine had always made it a point to be up front about her sexuality any time male colleagues took an interest in her. She didn't have enough energy to put up with raging male hormones, and she preferred honesty over the closet. Don Garrett, however, had taken a little longer than most to get the complete picture.

At first he refused to believe her, but once he saw how serious she was he took it upon himself to try to change her mind. He gave up dating anyone else for two months and considered that in itself a true sacrifice. He called her constantly and even showed up at her apartment one night.

"My cousin Bruno's on his way over here to explain what *leave me alone* means," Elaine had said when she found him outside her apartment. He finally left after thirty seconds of pleading and having the door slammed in his face.

But Don's persistence was both admirable and annoying. He'd kept up the pursuit through the summer that first year and didn't even *begin* to get the message until Maxine Weston and her lover came up from Boston for a visit in early October. Maxine, in her own no-nonsense way, was able to put it into words Don could finally understand.

Elaine, Maxine, and Maxine's new lover had gone to dinner at a nice Italian restaurant owned by Elaine's Uncle Tony. Maxine held her lover's hand quite openly through most of the evening and flirted with Elaine's cousin Angie at every opportunity. They were all drinking wine and having a good time when Don Garrett showed up out of nowhere and joined them. Things were going well until Maxine noticed Don slip an arm around Elaine's shoulder. Elaine politely asked him to remove it, which he did, but the mood had suddenly changed. Maxine looked Dr. Donald Garrett in the eye and said very simply, without benefit of lowering her voice, "You have a dick. Elaine doesn't like dicks. Whether yours is the biggest or the prettiest doesn't matter, Don. It's still a dick." She pointed her fork at him and said, "Get rid of the dick and you'll improve your chances. Do you understand what I'm saying?"

He turned a nice shade of red and nodded dumbly. More wine was poured, and they resumed their evening with some uncomfortable napkin arranging. The next day Don apologized, and eventually he and Elaine became good friends. He was happily married now, and he and Elaine often talked about interesting cases they came across. They also made it a point to try to attend the same conferences every year.

"How's Maxine?" he asked with a grin. His dark hair was beginning to thin on top, but he'd kept in shape and had that million-dollar smile. "Still telling it like it is?"

"Some things will never change," Elaine said.

Don congratulated her again on her paper and then took a moment to study her more closely. He sipped his coffee and squinted thoughtfully. "You look different. Happier maybe. What's going on with you these days?"

"I'm in love," she said, and then broke out into a silly grin. "Jesus, Don. I'd give anything to skip the rest of this conference and just catch the next plane home."

"So what's stopping you? Your part's over."

Elaine tilted her head as the suggestion began to seriously take hold. *He's right. What's stopping me? Change my reservations . . . get the next flight out. I could be at Cheryl's house in a matter of hours.*

"I'll do it," she said, deciding just like that. "Consider me outta here. Hurry up and finish your lunch."

Don laughed and poked at his french fries. He popped one in his mouth and smiled. "I guess you're still into women then."

Elaine raised an eyebrow and smirked. "And I guess you still have a dick."

Cheryl fed Cardigan a nice chunk of mackerel and mentally went over her meeting with the city manager earlier that day. She had gotten him to admit that money in the budget could be juggled if the public didn't like the suggested cuts in library hours, but he didn't promise anything. Cheryl knew what had to be done to get the public's attention on this. After leaving the city manager's office, she'd spent the rest of the afternoon and most of the evening in a meeting with the head librarians of all the branches in the city. They had work to do and petitions to circulate.

Cheryl checked the clock on the stove; it was eight-thirty already. She wondered what Elaine was doing right then and remembered her mentioning a banquet when they'd talked that morning. Cheryl reached down and rubbed Cardigan between the ears as he sniffed the mackerel and flicked his tail in appreciation.

The doorbell rang, and she went to answer it. She turned the porch light on and peeked through the drapes to find Mickey standing there. She was instantly furious.

"Open the door!"

She's been drinking, Cheryl thought as her anger subsided a bit.

"Open the goddamned door!"

Cheryl unlocked the door, and Mickey shoved it open and stumbled inside.

"Yes, I've been drinking and driving," Mickey said in answer to an unspoken question. "Barhopping via public transportation just don't cut it."

The next thing Cheryl knew Mickey was leaning against the wall with her hands covering her face, crying and mumbling. "I've really fucked things up. Is she here? Her car's not out front. And that bitch Veronica! She's making me crazy. Oh, fuck. I need to sit down." She stumbled over to the sofa and sprawled across it on her back.

"Why didn't you call your AA sponsor?" Cheryl snapped.

"Don't start with me!" Mickey yelled, flinging her arms and trying to sit up. Exhausted, she quit struggling with herself and propped her head up on the end of the sofa in what had to be an uncomfortable position. "And my mother! Don't tell my mother anything about this. Or Phoebe either. They already think I'm a fuckup. I had a few drinks," she said. She tried to get up again but collapsed with a thud. "I had a few drinks. What's the big deal?" She was mumbling again, but at least beginning to wind down. "I can't let em see me this way . . . I can't let em . . . oh, fuck." A few seconds later she passed out.

Cheryl sat down across from her and dialed the number for Mickey's AA sponsor. She knew it by heart from the last time Mickey had fallen off the wagon. After several rings, Cheryl left a message on the answering machine, sat back, and tried to sort through her feelings.

With a sense of relief, she realized that the anger she'd nurtured for weeks was finally gone. Cheryl, watching Mickey sleep with her mouth slightly open and an arm dangling over her head, was sad and felt empty. There was a flicker of compassion for the Mickey who couldn't give up alcohol, but other than that Cheryl was at a loss to feel much of anything. Their life together had been a sham. Mickey had never really loved her, and Cheryl knew that now. *But*, she thought, *I was in love with her, so what's happening here? How can I turn it off so quickly? One minute everything's fine, and the next I don't care if I ever see her again.*

Cheryl was well aware that it had everything to do with how her real parents had abandoned her as a child. Years of therapy had helped resolve some of those issues, but the little girl whose biological parents had left her to the state of Texas was still there somewhere — just as frightened and angry as ever. Comparing Mickey to the two people who'd given her away wasn't fair to Mickey, but Cheryl found herself doing it anyway. In Cheryl's mind, neglecting a child and cheating on a lover were similar. Both acts were shrouded in selfishness and total disregard for anyone else. It all reeked of me, me, me, and Cheryl hated it. For a while Mickey's betrayal had hurt just as deeply as Cheryl's having to watch a social worker stuff her meager possessions in a paper bag before taking her off to a foster home. Cheryl knew that if as a six-year-old, she had gotten through that, she could survive anything, including Mickey Marcaluso running off to Mexico with a new lover.

And that's *why you can shut it off so easily,* she thought. *You deserve better than this, so stop worrying about it.*

She stretched out in her favorite chair and finally let herself think about Elaine. Cheryl hoped to be getting a phone call later after the banquet. Her gaze drifted over to Mickey's undignified pose on the sofa — mouth open, softly snoring. Cheryl compared Elaine with Mickey. They were physically similar, both very attractive women with thick, jet black hair and startling gray eyes. But that was where the similarities ended. Whereas Mickey was selfish and moody, Elaine was warm and amusing. Elaine's compassion and insight were a nice change from Mickey's continuous, cynical whining. There were so many things about Elaine that Cheryl was looking forward to exploring further. *But how can I think I'm falling in love with her so soon?* she wondered. *I'm still tossing Mickey's favorite snacks in the shopping cart and looking for her toothbrush in the bathroom every morning.*

The telephone rang and shook her from her reverie. Cheryl recognized Blanche's voice immediately.

"Please forgive me if this question is out of line," Blanche said, "but I just received the strangest phone call from Veronica. Is Mickey there with you by chance?"

"Passed out cold on the sofa," Cheryl said slowly. She was angry again, and it had come on so quickly that it caught them both by surprise. "Do you get this a lot, Blanche? Mickey's lovers calling you in the middle of the night wondering where she is?"

"Uh . . ."

"I'm so tired of this."

"I know," Blanche said with a sigh. "I'm sorry. We'll come over and get her."

"She was driving, Blanche." Her anger simmered away as she glared at Mickey again . . . Mickey who knew better than most how deadly alcohol and a vehicle could be . . . Mickey who had always poked fun at Cheryl's hatred for it. The Trinidads had died in a head-on collision with a drunk driver. Cheryl found it so easy to transfer her outrage over this incident to anyone choosing to be that irresponsible.

"We'll be right over," Cheryl heard Blanche say quietly before she hung up.

Cheryl no more than set the phone back on the table when it rang again. This time it was Betty Harris, Mickey's AA sponsor.

"Passed out cold on the sofa," Cheryl reported in a monotone.

"She called me once this week," Betty said. "I thought we'd talked it all out."

"Obviously not."

"I'm on my way."

"Never mind. Her mother's coming to get her."

"All the more reason for me to be there."

Cheryl hung the phone up and again set it on the coffee table, but before she could get comfortable in her chair once more, the doorbell rang. *If Veronica shows up here I swear to God I'll throw them* both

113

out! She yanked the drapes aside and saw Elaine standing there on the porch. Cheryl's surprise quickly turned to relief and delight.

She fumbled with the lock and pulled the door open. Elaine looked up with those electrifying gray eyes swimming in tears. She took a deep breath as if to compose herself and waited for Cheryl to drag her inside.

"What are you doing here?" Cheryl asked as she closed the door and put her arms around her. "This is a wonderful surprise."

Cheryl hugged her and then stepped back, keeping her hands on Elaine's shoulders. "What's wrong? Are you crying?" She touched Elaine's chin with a fingertip and tilted her head up a little. Just then the doorbell rang again and made them both jump. Cheryl opened it without benefit of checking to see who was there and found Veronica on the porch in a long black skirt with a matching jacket. Her blonde mass of Farrah Fawcett hair was as perfect as always. Cheryl yanked the door open wider.

"How long has Mickey been here?" Veronica asked. She was inside now, ignoring Cheryl but giving Elaine a very thorough once-over. "You *have* to be a Marcaluso," she said with a lecherous smile. "I'll have to make sure Mickey lets her hair grow out in the future." She finally took her eyes off Elaine long enough to turn back to Cheryl. "Where is she?"

"In the living room. Blanche is coming to get her." Cheryl watched as Elaine and Veronica both moved to the end of the sofa where Elaine abruptly turned away to stare at the bookcase across the room.

"She only had two drinks," Veronica said. "I went to the —"

"You knew she was drinking?" Cheryl asked.

"We were out with a group from work. Mickey's a big girl. She should know what she can and can't do."

The doorbell rang again. As Cheryl went to answer it she saw Elaine in the hallway heading toward the kitchen. *Will this night ever end?* Cheryl wondered.

Blanche and Phoebe came in dressed in sweatpants, high-tops, and baggy T-shirts. Blanche hugged her and apologized.

"Isn't that Elaine's car out front?" Phoebe asked.

Cheryl nodded. "She's in the kitchen."

"It's not like we tied her to a chair and forced drinks down her throat," Veronica said defensively. She reached over and gave Mickey a little shake, which did nothing but momentarily stop her from snoring. "Wake up, babe. Let's go home."

Blanche and Cheryl looked at each other. They both knew that the only way Mickey was going *anywhere* was if someone carried her.

Phoebe leaned against the doorjamb in the kitchen and waited for Elaine to finish making a pot of coffee.

"How's the skin business, Doc?" Phoebe asked.

"Flaky at best."

"Aren't you supposed to be in Saint Louis?"

"I was," Elaine said.

"How'd the paper go?"

"Good. There was some interesting feedback."

Phoebe went farther into the kitchen and stood beside her with hands clasped behind her back. They watched the coffeepot slowly fill up.

"You've been crying," Phoebe said. "Care to talk about it?"

"Not really."

"You sure?"

"Positive. It's nothing."

"You leave a conference early — a conference you've been looking forward to for three months. You show up at your sister's ex-lover's house at nine o'clock on a Saturday night, and you've been crying. That's a bit more than nothing."

Elaine didn't say anything as they both continued to watch the coffeepot.

"Is something going on between you and Cheryl?" Phoebe asked. "Please tell me no. I hate lying to your mother."

The doorbell rang again as Elaine got three cups out of the cabinet.

"Now who could *that* be?" Phoebe grumbled. She fixed Blanche a cup of coffee and another for herself. She took the third cup Elaine had carefully prepared and set it on a tray with the other two.

"This one's for Cheryl," Elaine said.

"You already know how she likes her coffee?"

Elaine offered a shy smile. "She talks in her sleep, too. I'm going home. I'll see you later."

Phoebe followed her out of the kitchen and down the hall to the living room. She delivered the other two cups of coffee, one each to Blanche and Cheryl, and reported that there was plenty more in the kitchen if anyone else wanted some.

Cheryl held her cup and took a cautious sip before noticing Elaine opening the front door. She set her coffee down on the table and went after her.

"Hey," she called over the ruckus. Blanche, Veronica, and Betty were now arguing about where the still passed-out Mickey would be spending the night. Cheryl reached for Elaine's arm and caught her before she was off the porch.

"Where are you going?" She pulled her back inside and glanced over at the noisy scene in the living room. She led Elaine back down the hallway to the kitchen.

"Where were you going?" Cheryl asked. She brought Elaine's hand up to her lips for a kiss.

"Home, I think."

"Home?" Cheryl said, surprised. "You've been crying!"

Embarrassed, Elaine tried to look away from her, but Cheryl wasn't having any of it. With the tip of a finger under Elaine's chin, Cheryl raised her head up. "You're hurting. Tell me what's happened."

Elaine blinked back tears, but before she could find her voice, Cheryl had come to a conclusion of her own.

"You saw Mickey's car here," she said. "Is that what this is all about?"

Elaine looked straight ahead and took a deep, ragged breath.

"My god, Elaine. What were you expecting to find?"

"We've never really talked about Mickey before," Elaine said in a hoarse whisper.

"What were you thinking when you saw her car?" Cheryl asked with an edge of anger in her voice. "That I'd waited until you left town before seeing her again? That we were making love? What? Tell me."

Elaine closed her eyes and visibly trembled at both suggestions. Pulling up in front of the house and finding Mickey's car there . . . All Elaine had been able to think about at the time was the look on Mickey's face that day in her office, the look that had confirmed Mickey's true feelings for Cheryl. And then her car was there in front of Cheryl's house, and Elaine remembered thinking, *I should've called first. Why didn't I call?* The tears, however, had been unexpected, giving her no warning until after she'd already rung the doorbell.

"Cheryl," boomed a voice at the kitchen door. "Can you talk to these people out here?"

Both Cheryl and Elaine were startled by the interruption. Cheryl searched Elaine's face with a stern expression and said, "Don't move." Enunciating each word slowly, she added, "I'll be right back."

Cheryl was out of the kitchen, following an older woman Elaine had never seen before. She could hear Cheryl's voice over everyone else's in the living room.

"I don't care where Mickey goes or who she goes with, just get her out of here."

There was a moment of total silence before the buzz of arguing voices started up again. From the kitchen Elaine could hear bits and pieces of phrases through the bedlam — *take her feet, where are my keys, she belongs with her lover, get the door, she belongs with her mother, watch her head, Christ, she's heavy.* A few minutes later Elaine heard the front door close, and then Cheryl reappeared in the kitchen.

"They left," Cheryl said and slowly came over to stand in front of her again. Their eyes met, and they were suddenly very aware of each other.

"How could you think I'd rather be with someone else after the way it's been between us?" Cheryl asked. She crossed her arms over her chest. "My memories of Mickey aren't very pleasant, Elaine. When I think of her I see the person who'd rather blame her problems on someone else. I see the person who can only think of herself no matter what the situation is. I see the woman who ran off to Mexico with the first person who came along." Cheryl tossed a stray lock of hair away from her eyes and lowered her voice. "I keep asking myself if this is normal. If all this anger and negative energy is a good thing." She reached over and brushed away a tear that had scampered down Elaine's cheek. "All I really know right now is that I like being with you. I like it very much. I'm probably even falling in love with you, but I'm not ready to admit that yet." She caressed Elaine's cheek with the back of her hand. "Your perfume was still on my pillow last night," she whispered. "And I wanted you there with me more than anything."

Elaine leaned over and kissed her, a slow, deep breathtaking kiss that left them both weak with desire. Cheryl put her arms around Elaine's neck and whispered, "I've missed you, and I'm glad you're back. Now please come to bed with me."

Chapter Eleven

Monday morning Mickey was waiting for Elaine when she arrived at the office. *She looks like hell,* Elaine thought as she slipped on a clean lab coat.

"Ten minutes of your time," Mickey said. Her face was drawn, and she looked as though she hadn't gotten much sleep the night before. But her clothes were impeccable. She was dressed for court in a dark blue skirt and jacket, pale blue silk blouse, and matching heels. What she lacked in personality she made up for in appearance.

Elaine opened the door to her small office and

motioned toward the chair in front of her desk. "When did you pick up your car?"

"Yesterday afternoon," Mickey said. "Phoebe drove me over."

Elaine noticed how Mickey avoided looking at her and decided that she was probably embarrassed about Saturday night. Elaine chose not to make it any worse for her than it already was.

Mickey cleared her throat and popped her neck in that irritating little ritual she always went through when she was nervous. "I ... uh ..." she started and then drummed her fingers on the arm of the chair. "Can you give Cheryl a message for me?" she asked. Not waiting for a reply, she said, "Tell her I'm going into therapy and I'm attending AA meetings once a day. And tell her I'm sorry for everything. Veronica and Cancun ... everything. Just tell her that."

"Why'd you go to her house on Saturday?" Elaine asked.

"Why?" Mickey repeated, surprised by the question. "I think I was looking for you, actually. To see if you'd be there. I don't know. I don't remember much." She tugged on her skirt and sat up straighter in her chair. "Look, I know she doesn't want to see me or talk to me right now, but there's a definite message in all that somewhere. Doesn't it tell you something?"

"It tells me she doesn't want to see you or talk to you."

"That's it? That's the best you can do? She's rebounding, Elaine. She's pissed at me, and she knows which buttons to push. She's just using you, but she won't stay pissed forever. All this will blow over. Can't you see that?"

"And in the meantime it's my car in her driveway and my sneakers under her bed," Elaine said simply. "Do you really think we should be having this conversation?"

Mickey glared at her with a look of pure rage.

"I'll deliver your message," Elaine said.

"You do that." Mickey stood up and put her hands on the edge of Elaine's desk and leaned forward. "She still loves me. That'll never change."

Elaine shrugged and stood up too, stuffing her hands in her lab coat pockets, matching Mickey's height inch for inch. "We'll see."

Elaine paid for the pizza and tipped the delivery man. She scanned Cheryl's living room for Cardigan and Noah, making sure they were getting along okay. At Cheryl's suggestion Elaine had brought Noah over for a trial run at cohabitation. So far the cats were staying out of each other's way, but both Cheryl and Elaine were ready in case fur should begin to fly.

"Mickey came to see me today," Elaine said as she set the pizza on the table. Elaine didn't want to bring any of this up, but she'd made a promise to Mickey. She opened the box and saw the anchovies on the pizza. "I can't believe you like anchovies. This is great. How's your brussels sprout threshold? And liver? Do you like either of those?"

"I like them both, as a matter of fact," Cheryl said.

"Hmm. Interesting." *Yes,* Elaine thought. *Neither one of us wants to talk about Mickey.* They sat down to eat, and Elaine savored an anchovy-laced bite before continuing. She had, after all, promised to relay the message. "Mickey came by my office and wanted me to tell you she's starting therapy and going back to AA. And she says she's sorry about the Mexico thing. She just wanted you to know."

"And now I know. Thanks." Cheryl nodded toward Noah and Cardigan sniffing at an ivy leaf, no doubt having gotten a whiff of anchovy in the air. "They seem to be doing okay."

"Yes, they do," Elaine agreed.

"With Noah staying here now, you won't have any excuse not to bring more of your things over," Cheryl said.

"Have I been making excuses?"

Cheryl laughed and trimmed a piece of crust with a nibble. "No, not really. I'd like you to think about moving in with me. You're here every night anyway. We might as well make it official."

Elaine nonchalantly set her pizza slice down so Cheryl wouldn't see her hand shaking. "We'd be like housemates who sleep together?" Elaine asked. She reached into the pizza box to get another slice even though she already had one on her plate. "Or is this your way of asking me to marry you?"

Cheryl's slight smile made Elaine's pulse begin to race. Elaine pulled an anchovy off and tossed it in her mouth. She shrugged and said, "I guess it's kind of silly to talk about our getting married when you're not even sure if you love me yet." She picked up her wineglass with a semisteady hand and took a generous sip. "So I guess we'll just be housemates who sleep together." Setting her glass down again, Elaine slowly ran a fingertip around the rim. "I still get to sleep with you if I move in, don't I?"

"What the hell are you talking about?" Cheryl asked in exasperation. Elaine's eyes flew open. She'd never heard Cheryl cuss before.

"I don't need a housemate," Cheryl said, "and why would I make love with you now and not after you've moved in?" She got another piece of pizza from the box and dropped it on her plate. "And yes, to answer your earlier question. This is my way of asking you to marry me."

"Would you marry someone you're not in love with?"

That exasperated look had returned as her eyes searched Elaine's face, but then suddenly Cheryl's expression softened and she leaned back in her chair. "Are you serious?" she asked.

"Forget I said anything," Elaine whispered. She had no idea where her voice had gone, and to her horror she felt a rush of tears on the way. *I'm pushing her for answers that she doesn't have. What's the matter with me?* "Please. Forget it."

"Elaine," Cheryl said. "Darling. I think I've been in love with you ever since that hundred-dollar kiss you gave me." She smiled and slowly reached across the table for her hand. Cheryl's voice was low and full of emotion as she said, "That day at Gay Fiesta. I was really nervous when I saw you get in the kissing booth line. I already had some very strong feelings for you by then." She looked up and laughed softly at another memory. "And then there you were in front of me, checking out the mouthwash and chatting with Joey. I could tell you were nervous too, and it made me want you even that much more." She laughed again. "Then your beeper went off. Remember that?" Her eyes met Elaine's in a

124

searching, penetrating gaze, and Elaine's stomach did a new series of cartwheels. "But beeper or no beeper, Dr. Marcaluso, you weren't going *any*where that day until I got my kiss."

Elaine nodded and squeezed her hand. "I don't even remember driving to the hospital afterward."

Cheryl laughed and propped her elbows on the table.

"So," Elaine whispered, grateful that her voice had returned, "are we getting married or not? The pizza's getting cold."

Elaine missed Maxine at breakfast the next morning. She'd been in surgery delivering twins. Elaine decided to stop by Maxine's office after work and was immediately thankful that she'd lost interest in obstetrics early on in medical school. The waiting room was overflowing with women in different stages of pregnancy — some resting their magazines on huge round bellies and hoping to someday be able to see their feet again. Almost all were fanning themselves in the relatively cool office. Elaine stopped in front of the framed sign in the waiting area and shook her head. In bold letters she read: CONFUCIUS SAY: SHE WHO WAIT IN DOCTOR'S OFFICE MUST BE PATIENT.

"Sorry about breakfast," Maxine said to her a few minutes later as she handed a chart to the nurse. "I can spare you three minutes while I change shoes. My feet are screaming for sneakers."

"Check your schedule for a night that you and Betina are free for dinner," Elaine said once they were in Maxine's office. "Not anywhere very public, though. I don't want you two sneaking off in some crowded restaurant and having sex in the kitchen or something."

"Aren't you the little puritan all of a sudden," Maxine said with a light laugh. "How about whipping up one of those Italian feasts you're famous for? Have you cooked anything for Cheryl yet?"

"No, now that you mention it."

"You're not publicizing your best qualities, Dr. Marcaluso. How's she ever going to know what a deal she's getting?"

Elaine smiled. "She knows."

Maxine finished tying her shoe and raked her fingers through her wild hair. She looked tired. "Your three minutes are up. I'll call you with a date that's good for us."

Elaine adjusted a burner and then peeked in the oven just as the doorbell rang. She went to let Cheryl in and was momentarily speechless when she saw her in an ankle-length skirt with a soft gold flower-and-stamp print, a white long-sleeve blouse, and a beige vest.

My lover the librarian is a knockout, Elaine thought as she closed the door and kissed her. Cheryl's gently-probing tongue sent a surge of energy through Elaine's entire body.

Cheryl draped her arms around Elaine's neck and said, "It smells like your mother's house in here. That's a huge compliment, by the way."

"I think so too. Thanks."

"I didn't know you could cook."

Elaine tilted her head back as Cheryl's lips explored her throat. "I'm Italian. My talents are many."

"Mmm. Yes, I've noticed." Cheryl ran her hands down the front of Elaine's sweater. "You need help with anything?"

"Getting you out of these clothes, maybe," she whispered.

After dinner the four of them collapsed in Elaine's living room. Maxine and Betina held hands on the sofa while Cheryl and Elaine cuddled on the love seat across from them. They had all eaten too much and were waiting a while before sampling the Italian dream cake Elaine had for dessert.

The lesbian community in San Antonio had made it possible for Cheryl's politically active path to cross both Maxine's and Betina's on many occasions. Elaine was surprised to learn that Cheryl and Betina had actually worked together on a voter registration drive during the first Clinton campaign.

"Joey from the kissing booth is Betina's brother," Cheryl explained to Elaine. "You remember the kissing booth, don't you?"

"Vividly."

Betina set her Diet Coke on the end table and tugged at a dangling earring. "Let's talk about sex," she said suddenly. Her smile was contagious and her enthusiasm refreshing. "I like talking about it almost as much as I like doing it." She gave Maxine's hand a pat and asked in a low, seductive voice, "Where's the most unusual place we've done it, darling?"

"The ambulance with the sirens going," Maxine said without hesitation. "What a rush *that* was, so to speak."

"Oh, yes. That *was* fun."

An ambulance? Cheryl mouthed to Elaine. They both raised their eyebrows, truly impressed.

"Shamu Stadium was nice too," Betina said. "I also liked that little incident on your riding lawnmower a few weeks ago."

"Oh, and don't forget the reptile house at the zoo," Maxine said, fanning herself with an imaginary fan. "Holy moly."

Elaine snorted. "I don't believe a *fraction* of the things you tell me, Dr. Weston," she said. "If things were really that hot, then you wouldn't have to talk about it so much."

"Ooh," Betina cooed as she squirmed convincingly. "Talking about it just makes it that much *hotter!*"

Cheryl had spent most of Wednesday morning on the phone checking with other librarians on how the petition drive was going. They made plans to meet at the main library on Thursday night for another brainstorming session. A while later someone brought Cheryl a message that said Janet Landro wanted to meet her for lunch. Cheryl glanced at her watch and saw that she had five minutes to get to the restaurant.

Janet had a table in the back and was waving her menu in the air when Cheryl arrived.

"Your line was busy all morning," she complained. "I wasn't sure you'd gotten my message."

"This new city budget has me running," Cheryl said as she opened her menu. She was tired of thinking about it. She ordered the special and squeezed a lemon wedge into her water glass.

"Guess who I had dinner with last night?" Janet said. Not waiting for an answer, she blurted, *"Mickey.* We ran into each other at a coffee shop and spent two hours bitching about Veronica. Mickey says you're seeing someone else, by the way. Why didn't you tell me?"

Cheryl just looked at her in total disbelief.

"I know this thing with me sleeping with Veronica again upset you a little," Janet continued. "And then I heard that Veronica was seeing someone else while she was sleeping with Mickey *and* me. Jesus. What's Veronica's problem anyway? She was never like this before." She paused as the waitress set their plates down. "Mickey misses you, Cheryl. She talks about you all the time."

"I don't believe this," Cheryl said. "The woman skipped town with your lover, Janet — with tickets that were bought for *your* birthday, no less."

"Don't remind me. Hey, everybody makes mistakes. She's having a rough time right now."

"So what? Who cares?"

"She misses you."

"Mickey never missed me when it counted," Cheryl said. "I've gone on with my life. What's the matter with you? How can you associate with someone like that? She slept with your *lover*, for crissakes. Where's your pride?"

"Hey. Fuck pride. I learned a long time ago that pride won't keep you warm at night."

Cheryl fluffed up her mashed potatoes with lethal, jabbing fork action. "I'd rather freeze to death."

Chapter Twelve

Cheryl put the last of the dirty dishes in the dishwasher and listened as Elaine lectured the cats about walking across the answering machine. A few minutes later Elaine came up behind her and pressed her body against Cheryl's back.

"Are you sure you have room for me here?" Elaine asked. "I've got lots of stuff."

"We'll make room."

The telephone rang, and Cheryl answered it. Blanche was on the other end wanting to know if she and Phoebe could come over.

"I just made a pound cake," she said. "It's still warm."

Cheryl smiled. "The coffee'll be ready when you get here." She hung up and put her arms around Elaine's neck. "That was your mother. They're coming over. I wonder what's up? Have you told her about us yet?"

"No. I haven't had a chance."

Elaine was a little nervous as she set cups and dessert plates out on the table a while later. Phoebe and her mother had just arrived; she could hear them in the living room with Cheryl as the three of them talked about how best to rearrange certain furniture.

"My daughter the doctor's here," Blanche said with surprise when she saw Elaine in the dining room. "I didn't notice your car out front."

"You were too busy swooning over that cake," Phoebe said with a wink. "Hey, Doc. How's the skin business?"

"The usual rash of patients," Elaine said. "So what brings you two out?"

"Your sister," Blanche said. "My daughter the lawyer went to confession today." She set the cake down with a flourish in the middle of the table and pulled out a chair. "She's been going to those AA meetings too. I think she's really gonna do it this time. She's talking seriously about cleaning up her act." Blanche looked over at Cheryl, waiting for her to say something.

"I'll get a knife," Phoebe said.

"Bring me one too," Cheryl stated dryly.

Phoebe chuckled. "I meant for the cake."

Cheryl rubbed the bridge of her nose as if attempting to ease a headache.

"Well?" Blanche said. "She's really trying. Mickey hasn't been to confession in fifteen years."

"I thought lawyers had to go once a day," Elaine said. "It's a rule or something, I think."

Phoebe came back with the knife and started cutting the cake.

"Why are you doing this, Blanche?" Cheryl asked. "Where does it say Mickey and I have to be friends? Where's it written that I have to forgive her for everything she's done? I don't care if she's in church every waking moment and never takes another drink as long as she lives, I don't want to *hear* about it, talk about it, or think about it. Can't you understand that?"

Slowly, Blanche looked at Phoebe, Elaine, and then Cheryl, one at a time. She eventually directed her next statement to her daughter the doctor. "Help me talk some sense into this woman. Your sister's trying to get her life back together."

"Why should I?" Elaine said. "Cheryl's right. Mickey had her chance — several chances, in fact — and blew every one of them."

"I agree," Phoebe said. "Mickey's been a shit. You can't expect Cheryl to just forget all that. You can't force them to be friends, honey. That could take years. Maybe longer, maybe never."

Elaine studied her mother for a moment and saw the disappointment on her face. *No, no, no,* Elaine thought as all four of them sat there pretending to eat cake and drink coffee. *She can't be. Not my mother.*

Elaine set her fork down and took a deep breath. "Mom," she said. "Are you trying to get Mickey and Cheryl back together?"

"That's entirely up to them," Blanche said. "I just think it's important that Cheryl know how hard Mickey's trying."

"But you'd like to see them together again."

"Elaine," Cheryl said, and reached for her hand.

Elaine felt heaviness in her chest just thinking about her mother taking Mickey's side this way and coming to her defense. She felt dizzy for a moment, but Cheryl's firm grip kept her anchored.

"Mom," Elaine said. "Why is it always Mickey you want to see happy? Don't I deserve to be happy too?"

"Of course you do," Blanche said, truly confused. "I want the best for *both* my kids. What kind of question is that? You know full well that Mickey's always needed a little guidance, a little push in the right direction. If we wait around for *her* to figure it out, she'll *really* screw things up."

"That's fine," Elaine said, "but this time you need to guide her in some other direction. Any direction other than Cheryl's. It's your daughter the doctor who's in love with Cheryl now, and I'm here to stay."

Blanche's eyes widened in surprise as she stared at her. "You and Cheryl?"

Elaine nodded and brought Cheryl's hand up to her lips and kissed it.

Blanche shot a look across the table at Phoebe. "Did you know about this?" she barked.

"Sort of, but not really," Phoebe said.

"What kind of answer is that?" Blanche sat back in her chair and suddenly looked exhausted. "I'm sorry, baby. I didn't know. But now that I think about it, you've been here the last two times we've come over." She looked at them and frowned. "Why didn't you say something?" To Cheryl she asked, "Why didn't you tell us?"

"Maybe it's none of our business," Phoebe suggested diplomatically.

"Oh," Blanche said. "Well, I guess you're right. It's not, is it?"

Cheryl began to laugh and then squeezed Elaine's hand again before she let go of it. "This is all still new for us," she said. "I'm sure we'll eventually get around to it, but we're not quite at the talking stage yet."

"Oh," Blanche said. "And here we've been inviting ourselves over all the time." She looked down at the slice of untouched cake on her plate. "We're nothing but a pair of honeymoon crashers. Maybe we should get our cake to go, Phoebe dear."

"You'll do no such thing," Cheryl said. "This honeymoon could go on forever." She met Elaine's eyes across the table. "And I truly expect it to."

"Does Mickey know about this?" Blanche asked after a moment.

"Yes," Elaine said.

"That little shit," Blanche mumbled.

Even though Elaine had wanted to hire professional movers, Phoebe had convinced her that with Elaine's meager possessions it would be more trouble to hire movers than for them to do it themselves.

"It'll be fun," Phoebe kept assuring them.

On the day of the move, Cheryl instructed the

moving detail, which was composed of Blanche, Phoebe, Maxine, and Betina, on which boxes were ready to load onto Phoebe's truck. There were the don't-touch pile, the throw-away pile and the does-this-belong-to-anybody pile in the middle of Elaine's living room. Elaine had been called away to the hospital on an emergency earlier.

"Where's a woman in labor when I need her?" Maxine asked on her way out the door with her end of a coffee table.

"They wait until we're having magnificent sex before they page you, darlin'," Betina reminded her.

Cheryl and Blanche had everything in the kitchen boxed up and were getting ready to begin on Elaine's bedroom. Phoebe came in and gave Blanche a peck on the cheek.

"The truck's loaded," she said. "I'm taking Betina and Maxine with me to drop this stuff off." To Cheryl she said, "Are you sure you won't go so you can tell us where to put it?"

"Everything's labeled," Cheryl said. "If something's not clear, we'll fix it later. Let me give you my house key."

After the three left the telephone rang, and there was a moment of acute frustration when neither Cheryl nor Blanche could find it. Cheryl finally located the cord and pulled the phone out from under a stack of clean towels near the fireplace.

"Hello," she said breathlessly.

"Hi," Elaine said. "It's me." She lowered her voice and asked, "What are you wearing?

Cheryl laughed. "Sweat. I'm wearing sweat. Where are you?"

"I'm on my way. Do we need anything while I'm out? Sodas, ice, wine, pizza?"

"We're fine," Cheryl said. "Let me suggest that you don't dally, dearest. Maxine thinks you paged yourself so you'd get out of work."

"I had a real patient with a legitimate emergency," Elaine said. "That's my story, and I'm stickin' to it."

"Of course."

"Besides," Elaine continued, "the only reason Maxine would think that way is because that's what *she'd* do if we were moving *her*. Well, I'd better go and let you get back to work. I'll be there in a few minutes."

Cheryl hung up and set the phone down in plain view. Blanche was in the doorway leaning on a broom and watching her.

"That had to be my daughter the doctor," she said.

"It was. She's on her way."

Blanche nodded and propped the broom against the wall. "She makes you happy. I'm not sure I've ever seen you really happy before."

"You might be right," Cheryl admitted. "Elaine and I are a lot alike." She laughed and said, "Maxine thinks we're two of the most boring people she's ever known."

"There's nothing wrong with boring," Blanche said. "Phoebe and I've been boring for twenty-five years, and we like it fine." She picked up the stack of towels and put them in an empty box. "Mickey and Janet have been seeing a lot of each other lately. My worst fear with those two is that they'll both move in with Veronica and *really* screw themselves up."

"That wouldn't surprise me," Cheryl said. She followed Blanche into Elaine's bedroom and started taking the sheets off the bed. The telephone on the nightstand rang, and Cheryl reached over and answered it.

"Hi," Elaine said. "It's me again."

Cheryl smiled just hearing her voice. "Hi. Where are you?"

"I'm in the driveway."

"You're where?" Cheryl moved to the window and opened the curtains so she could see outside.

Elaine waved at her from the driver's seat and whispered into her cellular phone, "What are you wearing now?"

Everything was moved by six-thirty that evening, and only Blanche and Phoebe stayed to help them spruce up the old, empty apartment. Cheryl ached in places she didn't know she had and took a break after an hour of sweeping and vacuuming. She stretched out on the empty living room floor just for a moment and fell asleep. What seemed like only minutes later, she felt someone kissing her on the forehead. The light from the hallway cast a dim glow into the room, and Cheryl opened her eyes to find Elaine beside her.

"Hi," Cheryl said sleepily.

"You ready to go home?" Elaine asked. She moved her fingers through the front of Cheryl's hair to get it out of her face. "Everything's done."

"Everything? Where's Blanche and Phoebe?"

"I sent them home hours ago."

"What time is it?"

"Eleven-thirty," Elaine said. She leaned over and kissed her on the lips, and Cheryl was suddenly more awake than she realized. One small kiss turned into two, and the next thing Cheryl knew her body was stirring with arousal.

"I love you," Elaine whispered.

Cheryl slipped her hand around the back of Elaine's neck and pulled her closer for a deep, hungry kiss. She wanted to touch her everywhere and in return to feel Elaine's hands all over her own body. As if reading her mind, Elaine began unbuttoning Cheryl's shirt at the same time that Cheryl began tugging Elaine's over her head. The rustling of clothing and soft murmurs heightened their excitement as their mouths sought more of each other.

Cheryl helped get them both out of their clothes and wanted Elaine's cool, soft skin touching hers, rubbing hers. They pulled away from one another just long enough for Cheryl to see the desire in Elaine's eyes as she gazed down at her. Elaine let her long black hair fall forward and tease Cheryl's breasts for a moment. She then tossed her head back, and her hair cascaded past her bare shoulders.

"I love you too," Cheryl said. *God, how I love you.*

Elaine stayed next to her and rubbed her own hard nipples against the side of Cheryl's breast. They began kissing again, mouths open, tongues darting and probing, bodies writhing with eagerness. Cheryl felt Elaine's hand move between her legs where the most exquisite stroking began. Cheryl was ready for her with legs open and hips moving in a steady rhythm.

Elaine broke away from the kiss and directed her attention to Cheryl's breasts where she circled swollen nipples with her tongue before taking one in her mouth. The pressure increased between Cheryl's legs, and she was alive with a hot, pulsating sensation that took its glorious sweet time spreading through her body.

"Oh, yes . . ." Cheryl whispered urgently. Words and syllables were caught in her throat after that, and she tightened her arms around Elaine's neck. It was electrifying and powerful, like a swift current surging forward. Cheryl came with a long raspy groan and buried her face in Elaine's hair. She held her that way and trembled while fingers danced and touched her with measured precision. Cheryl felt Elaine's mouth leave her breast and then kiss her tenderly on the cheek.

Cheryl pulled Elaine on top of her, and opened her legs even farther as Elaine nestled between them. Elaine slowly rocked against Cheryl. She arched her back, reaching for that complete connection that had become so familiar. Cheryl was still sensitive and throbbing from all the stimulation, but she knew without a doubt that they would come together this time.

"You feel so good," she said in a ragged whisper. "Oh, god, Elaine . . . you feel so good."

She nuzzled Elaine's neck and matched the steady rocking with her hips. Their rhythm increased, and Cheryl grabbed and pulled Elaine closer in an urgent grip of passion as the heat unfolded. The first flutter of orgasm was like a warm liquid flowing through her, and seconds later the frantic thrill of intoxication flushed their bodies in one continuous rush of pleasure.

Elaine shuddered and collapsed on top of Cheryl, her face buried in Cheryl's neck and shoulder. Tiny kisses began at her earlobe where Elaine had very little strength to do anything else.

They trembled and attempted to resume normal breathing. Cheryl wrapped her legs around Elaine and rubbed Elaine's wetness into her own pulsating center one more time. Elaine kissed Cheryl's cheek with a bit more strength than before and then lay beside her, exhausted.

"That was fabulous," Cheryl said. She kissed the top of Elaine's head and brushed her cheek against her soft hair. She felt close to tears and was happier at that moment than she could ever remember being. "Where have you been all my life?" Cheryl asked in a quiet, faraway voice.

Elaine kissed her cheek and whispered, "Waiting for you."

The planning committee for the Texas Lesbian Conference was meeting at the Women's Resource Center Wednesday evening. Cheryl and Phoebe sat together on one of two sofas in the crowded room and talked about how many conference T-shirts they should order. Fund-raising was the hot topic of discussion for the evening with the same old tired suggestions mulled over. The planning committee was into the fine-tuning stage and accessing what loose ends needed to be tended to during the next few weeks. Cheryl was still amazed at how well the group was getting along.

After the meeting Phoebe and Cheryl volunteered to help clean up and were the last to leave. They locked the side door to the Resource Center, and Phoebe stuffed the key in her shorts pocket.

"Blanche is getting an award next week," Phoebe said. "Has Elaine mentioned anything about it?" She lowered the tailgate on her pickup and patted a place beside her for Cheryl to sit.

"For her work at the clinic," Cheryl said. "Yes. Elaine mentioned it."

"Good. Then I have a favor to ask you," Phoebe said.

The light from the street lit up the small, empty parking lot as Cheryl sat down next to her. She waited for Phoebe to continue and glanced over at her as Phoebe leaned her head back, letting her short blondish-gray hair touch the bottom of her collar. She looked tired and serious.

"You're a part of our family," Phoebe said. "A very important part. Blanche and I both think of you as one of our own." She reached for Cheryl's hand and gave it a motherly squeeze. "This favor I need won't be easy, and I don't like having to ask you, but I want you and Mickey to lay your differences aside for one evening and pretend that things are okay between you. I want you both to be at the awards banquet. Elaine too, of course. I know it would make Blanche happy to have all three of you there." Phoebe nervously drummed her fingers on the truck bed and looked straight ahead. "I had a long talk with Mickey this morning, and she's agreed to be on her best behavior. I also plan to have a similar discussion with Elaine tomorrow. Now talk to me, Cheryl. Can we make this happen?"

Cheryl sighed and hated being put in this position. She knew she'd have to say yes, but she still didn't like it.

"You know I'll be there," she said, and hopped off the tailgate. She started toward her car and called over her shoulder from the darkness, "That should give you some idea of how important Blanche is to me."

Blanche was surrounded by coworkers and board members and was having a splendid time. Cheryl smiled as she saw Elaine across the room once again being introduced to another group of suited strangers. The party room at the hotel was huge, and at last count a hundred and seventy-eight people were in attendance. Cheryl got herself another glass of punch and turned around just in time to run right into Mickey.

"Oh," Cheryl said, startled. "I'm sorry. Did I get any on you?"

"No," Mickey said as she brushed at the front of her jacket. "I don't think so. I've been wanting to talk to you," she said. "To apologize for showing up drunk at your house the other night. That was a stupid thing to do."

"What?" Cheryl said, sipping her punch. "Getting drunk or showing up at my house?"

"Both." Mickey shrugged and popped her neck in that irritating way that had always made Cheryl cringe. "I don't know what's the matter with me lately."

Cheryl glanced across the room again, searching for Elaine, who was with her mother and Phoebe in a small group of hospital administrators. Elaine looked up. Their eyes met and lingered before they both smiled. Elaine whispered something to her mother and began moving through the crowd toward Cheryl.

Cheryl left Mickey standing there talking by the punch bowl, and didn't bother to excuse herself. She had mingled enough and had given Blanche several opportunities to brag about and introduce her daughter the doctor to anyone and everyone even remotely interested. Cheryl decided that Elaine was now hers for the rest of the evening.

"Hi," Elaine said when they finally met in the middle of the room. "You look quite fetching tonight."

"So do you." Cheryl sipped her fruity punch and let her eyes slowly travel down Elaine's body. She was a beautiful woman, and Cheryl knew how lucky she was.

"If you don't stop looking at me that way I'll have to do something totally out of character," Elaine said.

"Mmm. Like what?"

"Like have my way with you right here." Elaine surveyed the immediate area with a quick glance and then lowered her voice and said, "On a table maybe. This one here. You with your head thrown back and breasts heaving. Your legs wrapped around me..."

"A scene that would surely make Betina and Maxine proud of us."

"Jesus," Elaine said, tugging on the collar of her blouse. "Why is it so hot in here all of a sudden?"

Cheryl laughed and slipped her arm around Elaine's waist. "Yes. I wonder why indeed."

LOOKING FOR NAIAD?

Buy our books at
www.naiadpress.com

or call our toll-free number
1-800-533-1973

or by fax (24 hours a day)
1-850-539-9731

THOSE WHO WAIT by Peggy J. Herring. 160 pp. Two
sisters . . . in love with the same woman.   ISBN 1-56280-223-2 $11.95

WHISPERS IN THE WIND by Frankie J. Jones. 192 pp. "If you
don't want this," she whispered, "all you have to say is 'stop.' "
ISBN 1-56280-226-7   11.95

WHEN SOME BODY DISAPPEARS by Therese Szymanski.
192 pp. 3rd Brett Higgins mystery.   ISBN 1-56280-227-5   11.95

THE WAY LIFE SHOULD BE by Diana Braund. 240 pp. Which
one will teach her the true meaning of love?   ISBN 1-56280-221-6   11.95

UNTIL THE END by Kaye Davis. 256pp. 3rd Maris Middleton
mystery.   ISBN 1-56280-222-4   11.95

FIFTH WHEEL by Kate Calloway. 224 pp. 5th Cassidy James
mystery.   ISBN 1-56280-218-6   11.95

JUST YESTERDAY by Linda Hill. 176 pp. Reliving all the
passion of yesterday.   ISBN 1-56280-219-4   11.95

THE TOUCH OF YOUR HAND edited by Barbara Grier and
Christine Cassidy. 304 pp. Erotic love stories by Naiad Press
authors.   ISBN 1-56280-220-8   14.95

WINDROW GARDEN by Janet McClellan. 192 pp. They discover
a passion they never dreamed possible.   ISBN 1-56280-216-X   11.95

PAST DUE by Claire McNab. 224 pp. 10th Carol Ashton
mystery.   ISBN 1-56280-217-8   11.95

CHRISTABEL by Laura Adams. 224 pp. Two captive hearts and
the passion that will set them free.   ISBN 1-56280-214-3   11.95

PRIVATE PASSIONS by Laura DeHart Young. 192 pp. An
unforgettable new portrait of lesbian love . . .   ISBN 1-56280-215-1   11.95

BAD MOON RISING by Barbara Johnson. 208 pp. 2nd Colleen
Fitzgerald mystery.   ISBN 1-56280-211-9   11.95

RIVER QUAY by Janet McClellan. 208 pp. 3rd Tru North
mystery. ISBN 1-56280-212-7 11.95

ENDLESS LOVE by Lisa Shapiro. 272 pp. To believe, once
again, that love can be forever. ISBN 1-56280-213-5 11.95

FALLEN FROM GRACE by Pat Welch. 256 pp. 6th Helen Black
mystery. ISBN 1-56280-209-7 11.95

THE NAKED EYE by Catherine Ennis. 208 pp. Her lover in the
camera's eye . . . ISBN 1-56280-210-0 11.95

OVER THE LINE by Tracey Richardson. 176 pp. 2nd Stevie
Houston mystery. ISBN 1-56280-202-X 11.95

JULIA'S SONG by Ann O'Leary. 208 pp. Strangely
disturbing . . . strangely exciting. ISBN 1-56280-197-X 11.95

LOVE IN THE BALANCE by Marianne K. Martin. 256 pp.
Weighing the costs of love . . . ISBN 1-56280-199-6 11.95

PIECE OF MY HEART by Julia Watts. 208 pp. All the
stuff that dreams are made of — ISBN 1-56280-206-2 11.95

MAKING UP FOR LOST TIME by Karin Kallmaker. 240 pp.
Nobody does it better . . . ISBN 1-56280-196-1 11.95

GOLD FEVER by Lyn Denison. 224 pp. By author of *Dream
Lover.* ISBN 1-56280-201-1 11.95

WHEN THE DEAD SPEAK by Therese Szymanski. 224 pp. 2nd
Brett Higgins mystery. ISBN 1-56280-198-8 11.95

FOURTH DOWN by Kate Calloway. 240 pp. 4th Cassidy James
mystery. ISBN 1-56280-205-4 11.95

A MOMENT'S INDISCRETION by Peggy J. Herring. 176 pp.
There's a fine line between love and lust . . . ISBN 1-56280-194-5 11.95

CITY LIGHTS/COUNTRY CANDLES by Penny Hayes. 208 pp.
About the women she has known . . . ISBN 1-56280-195-3 11.95

POSSESSIONS by Kaye Davis. 240 pp. 2nd Maris Middleton
mystery. ISBN 1-56280-192-9 11.95

A QUESTION OF LOVE by Saxon Bennett. 208 pp. Every
woman is granted one great love. ISBN 1-56280-205-4 11.95

RHYTHM TIDE by Frankie J. Jones. 160 pp. . . . to desire
passionately and be passionately desired. ISBN 1-56280-189-9 11.95

PENN VALLEY PHOENIX by Janet McClellan. 208 pp. 2nd
Tru North Mystery. ISBN 1-56280-200-3 11.95

BY RESERVATION ONLY by Jackie Calhoun. 240 pp. A
chance for true happiness. ISBN 1-56280-191-0 11.95

OLD BLACK MAGIC by Jaye Maiman. 272 pp. 9th Robin
Miller mystery. ISBN 1-56280-175-9 11.95

LEGACY OF LOVE by Marianne K. Martin. 240 pp. Women
will do anything for her . . . ISBN 1-56280-184-8 11.95

LETTING GO by Ann O'Leary. 160 pp. Laura, at 39, in love
with 23-year-old Kate.   ISBN 1-56280-183-X   11.95

LADY BE GOOD edited by Barbara Grier and Christine Cassidy.
288 pp. Erotic stories by Naiad Press authors. ISBN 1-56280-180-5   14.95

CHAIN LETTER by Claire McNab. 288 pp. 9th Carol Ashton
mystery.   ISBN 1-56280-181-3   11.95

NIGHT VISION by Laura Adams. 256 pp. Erotic fantasy romance
by "famous" author.   ISBN 1-56280-182-1   11.95

SEA TO SHINING SEA by Lisa Shapiro. 256 pp. Unable to resist
the raging passion . . .   ISBN 1-56280-177-5   11.95

THIRD DEGREE by Kate Calloway. 224 pp. 3rd Cassidy James
mystery.   ISBN 1-56280-185-6   11.95

WHEN THE DANCING STOPS by Therese Szymanski. 272 pp.
1st Brett Higgins mystery.   ISBN 1-56280-186-4   11.95

PHASES OF THE MOON by Julia Watts. 192 pp. . . . . hungry
for everything life has to offer.   ISBN 1-56280-176-7   11.95

BABY IT'S COLD by Jaye Maiman. 256 pp. 5th Robin Miller
mystery.   ISBN 1-56280-156-2   10.95

CLASS REUNION by Linda Hill. 176 pp. The girl from her
past . . .   ISBN 1-56280-178-3   11.95

DREAM LOVER by Lyn Denison. 224 pp. A soft, sensuous,
romantic fantasy.   ISBN 1-56280-173-1   11.95

FORTY LOVE by Diana Simmonds. 288 pp. Joyous, heart-
warming romance.   ISBN 1-56280-171-6   11.95

IN THE MOOD by Robbi Sommers. 160 pp. The queen of
erotic tension!   ISBN 1-56280-172-4   11.95

SWIMMING CAT COVE by Lauren Douglas. 192 pp. 2nd
Allison O'Neil Mystery.   ISBN 1-56280-168-6   11.95

THE LOVING LESBIAN by Claire McNab and Sharon Gedan.
240 pp. Explore the experiences that make lesbian love unique.
                                          ISBN 1-56280-169-4   14.95

COURTED by Celia Cohen. 160 pp. Sparkling romantic
encounter.   ISBN 1-56280-166-X   11.95

SEASONS OF THE HEART by Jackie Calhoun. 240 pp. Romance
through the years.   ISBN 1-56280-167-8   11.95

K. C. BOMBER by Janet McClellan. 208 pp. 1st Tru North
mystery.   ISBN 1-56280-157-0   11.95

LAST RITES by Tracey Richardson. 192 pp. 1st Stevie Houston
mystery.   ISBN 1-56280-164-3   11.95

EMBRACE IN MOTION by Karin Kallmaker. 256 pp. A whirlwind
love affair.   ISBN 1-56280-165-1   11.95

HOT CHECK by Peggy J. Herring. 192 pp. Will workaholic Alice
fall for guitarist Ricky?   ISBN 1-56280-163-5   11.95

OLD TIES by Saxon Bennett. 176 pp. Can Cleo surrender to a
passionate new love?   ISBN 1-56280-159-7   11.95

LOVE ON THE LINE by Laura DeHart Young. 176 pp. Will Stef
win Kay's heart?   ISBN 1-56280-162-7   11.95

DEVIL'S LEG CROSSING by Kaye Davis. 192 pp. 1st Maris
Middleton mystery.   ISBN 1-56280-158-9   11.95

COSTA BRAVA by Marta Balletbo Coll. 144 pp. Read the book,
see the movie!   ISBN 1-56280-153-8   11.95

MEETING MAGDALENE & OTHER STORIES by
Marilyn Freeman. 144 pp. Read the book, see the movie!
                                             ISBN 1-56280-170-8   11.95

SECOND FIDDLE by Kate 208 pp. 2nd P.I. Cassidy James
mystery.   ISBN 1-56280-169-6   11.95

LAUREL by Isabel Miller. 128 pp. By the author of the beloved
Patience and Sarah.   ISBN 1-56280-146-5   10.95

LOVE OR MONEY by Jackie Calhoun. 240 pp. The romance of
real life.   ISBN 1-56280-147-3   10.95

SMOKE AND MIRRORS by Pat Welch. 224 pp. 5th Helen Black
Mystery.   ISBN 1-56280-143-0   10.95

DANCING IN THE DARK edited by Barbara Grier & Christine
Cassidy. 272 pp. Erotic love stories by Naiad Press authors.
                                             ISBN 1-56280-144-9   14.95

TIME AND TIME AGAIN by Catherine Ennis. 176 pp. Passionate
love affair.   ISBN 1-56280-145-7   10.95

PAXTON COURT by Diane Salvatore. 256 pp. Erotic and wickedly
funny contemporary tale about the business of learning to live
together.   ISBN 1-56280-114-7   10.95

INNER CIRCLE by Claire McNab. 208 pp. 8th Carol Ashton
Mystery.   ISBN 1-56280-135-X   11.95

LESBIAN SEX: AN ORAL HISTORY by Susan Johnson.
240 pp. Need we say more?   ISBN 1-56280-142-2   14.95

WILD THINGS by Karin Kallmaker. 240 pp. By the undisputed
mistress of lesbian romance.   ISBN 1-56280-139-2   11.95

THE GIRL NEXT DOOR by Mindy Kaplan. 208 pp. Just what
you d expect.   ISBN 1-56280-140-6   11.95

NOW AND THEN by Penny Hayes. 240 pp. Romance on the
westward journey.   ISBN 1-56280-121-X   11.95

HEART ON FIRE by Diana Simmonds. 176 pp. The romantic and
erotic rival of *Curious Wine.*   ISBN 1-56280-152-X   11.95

DEATH AT LAVENDER BAY by Lauren Wright Douglas. 208 pp. 1st Allison O'Neil Mystery.
ISBN 1-56280-085-X 11.95

YES I SAID YES I WILL by Judith McDaniel. 272 pp. Hot romance by famous author.
ISBN 1-56280-138-4 11.95

FORBIDDEN FIRES by Margaret C. Anderson. Edited by Mathilda Hills. 176 pp. Famous author's "unpublished" Lesbian romance.
ISBN 1-56280-123-6 21.95

SIDE TRACKS by Teresa Stores. 160 pp. Gender-bending Lesbians on the road.
ISBN 1-56280-122-8 10.95

WILDWOOD FLOWERS by Julia Watts. 208 pp. Hilarious and heart-warming tale of true love.
ISBN 1-56280-127-9 10.95

NEVER SAY NEVER by Linda Hill. 224 pp. Rule #1: Never get involved with . . .
ISBN 1-56280-126-0 11.95

THE WISH LIST by Saxon Bennett. 192 pp. Romance through the years.
ISBN 1-56280-125-2 10.95

OUT OF THE NIGHT by Kris Bruyer. 192 pp. Spine-tingling thriller.
ISBN 1-56280-120-1 10.95

LOVE'S HARVEST by Peggy J. Herring. 176 pp. by the author of *Once More With Feeling*.
ISBN 1-56280-117-1 10.95

THE COLOR OF WINTER by Lisa Shapiro. 208 pp. Romantic love beyond your wildest dreams.
ISBN 1-56280-116-3 10.95

FAMILY SECRETS by Laura DeHart Young. 208 pp. Enthralling romance and suspense.
ISBN 1-56280-119-8 10.95

INLAND PASSAGE by Jane Rule. 288 pp. Tales exploring conventional & unconventional relationships.
ISBN 0-930044-56-8 10.95

DOUBLE BLUFF by Claire McNab. 208 pp. 7th Carol Ashton Mystery.
ISBN 1-56280-096-5 10.95

BAR GIRLS by Lauran Hoffman. 176 pp. See the movie, read the book!
ISBN 1-56280-115-5 10.95

THE FIRST TIME EVER edited by Barbara Grier & Christine Cassidy. 272 pp. Love stories by Naiad Press authors.
ISBN 1-56280-086-8 14.95

MISS PETTIBONE AND MISS McGRAW by Brenda Weathers. 208 pp. A charming ghostly love story.
ISBN 1-56280-151-1 10.95

CHANGES by Jackie Calhoun. 208 pp. Involved romance and relationships.
ISBN 1-56280-083-3 10.95

FAIR PLAY by Rose Beecham. 256 pp. An Amanda Valentine Mystery.
ISBN 1-56280-081-7 10.95

PAYBACK by Celia Cohen. 176 pp. A gripping thriller of romance, revenge and betrayal.
ISBN 1-56280-084-1 10.95

THE BEACH AFFAIR by Barbara Johnson. 224 pp. Sizzling summer romance/mystery/intrigue.
ISBN 1-56280-090-6 10.95

GETTING THERE by Robbi Sommers. 192 pp. Nobody does it like Robbi! ISBN 1-56280-099-X 10.95

FINAL CUT by Lisa Haddock. 208 pp. 2nd Carmen Ramirez Mystery. ISBN 1-56280-088-4 10.95

FLASHPOINT by Katherine V. Forrest. 256 pp. A Lesbian blockbuster! ISBN 1-56280-079-5 10.95

CLAIRE OF THE MOON by Nicole Conn. Audio Book — Read by Marianne Hyatt. ISBN 1-56280-113-9 16.95

FOR LOVE AND FOR LIFE: INTIMATE PORTRAITS OF LESBIAN COUPLES by Susan Johnson. 224 pp. ISBN 1-56280-091-4 14.95

DEVOTION by Mindy Kaplan. 192 pp. See the movie — read the book! ISBN 1-56280-093-0 10.95

SOMEONE TO WATCH by Jaye Maiman. 272 pp. 4th Robin Miller Mystery. ISBN 1-56280-095-7 10.95

GREENER THAN GRASS by Jennifer Fulton. 208 pp. A young woman — a stranger in her bed. ISBN 1-56280-092-2 10.95

TRAVELS WITH DIANA HUNTER by Regine Sands. Erotic lesbian romp. Audio Book (2 cassettes) ISBN 1-56280-107-4 16.95

CABIN FEVER by Carol Schmidt. 256 pp. Sizzling suspense and passion. ISBN 1-56280-089-1 10.95

THERE WILL BE NO GOODBYES by Laura DeHart Young. 192 pp. Romantic love, strength, and friendship. ISBN 1-56280-103-1 10.95

FAULTLINE by Sheila Ortiz Taylor. 144 pp. Joyous comic lesbian novel. ISBN 1-56280-108-2 9.95

OPEN HOUSE by Pat Welch. 176 pp. 4th Helen Black Mystery. ISBN 1-56280-102-3 10.95

ONCE MORE WITH FEELING by Peggy J. Herring. 240 pp. Lighthearted, loving romantic adventure. ISBN 1-56280-089-2 11.95

FOREVER by Evelyn Kennedy. 224 pp. Passionate romance — love overcoming all obstacles. ISBN 1-56280-094-9 10.95

WHISPERS by Kris Bruyer. 176 pp. Romantic ghost story. ISBN 1-56280-082-5 10.95

NIGHT SONGS by Penny Mickelbury. 224 pp. 2nd Gianna Maglione Mystery. ISBN 1-56280-097-3 10.95

These are just a few of the many Naiad Press titles — we are the oldest and largest lesbian/feminist publishing company in the world. We also offer an enormous selection of lesbian video products. Please request a complete catalog. We offer personal service; we encourage and welcome direct mail orders from individuals who have limited access to bookstores carrying our publications.